Legend of Fenrir

and other Nordic stories

PETER CURSON

ISBN-13: 978-0-9951548-5-8

Copyright © 2018 Peter Curson
All rights reserved. No part of this publication may be reproduced, distributed, or transmitted in any form or by any means, including photocopying, recording, or other electronic or mechanical methods, without the prior written permission of the publisher, except in the case of brief quotations embodied in critical reviews and certain other noncommercial uses permitted by copyright law.

All images licensed from Adobe Stock.

www.petercurson.com

Dedicated to He who reigns above
even the gods of Asgard

Contents

One	1
Two	17
Three	33
Four	45
Five	55
Six	65
Seven	78
Eight	82
Nine	98
Ten	105
Eleven	122
Twelve	132
Thirteen	148
Fourteen	161
Fifteen	172
Epilogue	177
Glossary of Characters	217
Glossary of Locations	223
Glossary of Norse Words	227
Glossary of Other Words	229

Legend of Fenrir

Part 1

ᚢᛁᛖ

ONE Is life unfair? Oftentimes it seems as such. Unfortunate things happen all the time to all people, not the least of which me. But to answer this, we must also ask is life fair? Do good things not also happen all the time to all people? Harsh winters plague some while bountiful harvests aid others. Death comes under the strike of sword or lash to the innocent and life is granted to those undeserving of it. What does it mean? Is life neither fair nor unfair, a sequence of connected yet impartial events that just simply happen? Or perhaps there is a force at work pushing these events to take place.

Some say there are three divine beings who dictate the happenings of all things in existence: the Three Norns. They sit at the bottom of Yggdrasil—the great World Tree that holds our worlds together and grants them life—and on its roots, they carve the destinies of all things and all people. Whatever the Norns carve, none can escape.

Fate.

Do I believe it?

Surely I have seen much stranger things in my life than

LEGEND OF FENRIR

three old crones carving designs on Yggdrasil's trunk, and indeed they may be there sitting amongst the roots, but I am in charge of my own fate. I, Fenrir, make my own decisions and I choose which paths to tread. And should those paths end in tragedy, it is through my own fault, not because of the Norns and not because life is unjust. It has taken me an entire year on Midgard's wide world to settle this within my heart, because when someone goes through an endless string of tragedies, when their resolve is chipped away with the strike of hammer and chisel without end until nothing is left but a shell of what they once were, their vision clears and they can finally see through the muck and mire. I cannot blame others or the world for my misfortune. I can only blame myself.

One year has passed since I escaped the gods of Asgard—the Æsir. Yes, escaped, because the Æsir captured me, took me from my home, and forced me to live with them where I could be watched and kept on a leash, forced to submit to their power and their way of life. I escaped their clutches, their captivity, when Odin, chief of the gods and ruler of Asgard, banished my twin sons from his realm, sending them to Midgard, world of the humans.

Why were they banished? Why was I captured? Simply put: we are Jötunn, of the world Jötunheim. The Æsir gods despise us Jötnar giants for they believe us inherently chaotic and reckless and stand against their very way of life. Our two races are opposite in everything; thus, if they are righteous then we are evil. If they are just then we are corrupt. However, more than they despise us, they fear us for we are strong.

The gods take comfort for they are protected by their elite: the High-Æsir. Odin and his sons. Hah. They are strong indeed, stronger than almost any Jötnar, but my sons and I have shown them that we too are powerful for we share a rare ability: shapeshifting.

A boon passed down from my father Loki, my sons

PETER CURSON

and I are able to change our forms into that of wolves, giant and menacing, larger than any beast that roams Midgard's world. I can eat a grown man whole I my wolf form. When we shift, our bodies grow, our senses sharpen, and our power multiplies beyond comprehension. Legions could stand against us and none would live to tell the tale. However, under the rule of the Æsir, trapped within their stone city and forced never to shift, we were never able to fully hone ourselves. But here on Midgard, we can become who we truly are for there are none who can stop us.

Sköll. Hati. My sons.

It has been one whole year since I have heard their voices and smelled their scents. The days before their banishment run through my mind every single day in this world. Oh, how we would wrestle and laugh, feast and be merry. When they were but small pups, they would stare at my wife Hyrrokkin and I as we told them grand stories of Jötnar heroes and the wars they fought and the power they possessed. And we reminded them that all Jötnar hold that power within their breasts, including them. Their eyes were wide with awe and amazement and I could see in them such great potential.

When they grew older, they would speak of these very stories with yearning in their hearts, yearning to go on their own quests that the *skalds* would one day speak of: two Jötunn men who committed feats of the greatest caliber that would be remembered for all of eternity. No Jötunn would go through life without hearing the names Sköll and Hati and the battles they won.

Alas, it did not turn out as such. They were born into Æsir oppression, and by that oppression they were banished from Asgard to spend their remaining days upon Midgard, forever removed from their people and their family. Why? They bested two of the High-Æsir in a jovial wrestling match. But it so happened to be the sons of Thor they bested. Thor, the

LEGEND OF FENRIR

Slayer of the Jötnar, the son of Odin who has caused more pain and hardship in my life than any other, save Odin himself. His persuasion played on Odin's fears leading to his decision to banish my sons, separating them from my wife and me. And now, a year after that tragic day, they are still lost to me. My wife remains in Jötunheim, our world, and I search endlessly for my son. For what other purpose is there now in life than to find them?

Hope dwindles. But it is not lost forever. If there is any comfort in the separation from my sons and my wife, if there is any silver-lining in my exile, it is found knowing that my sons are now free from captivity and oppression and that they live their own way on their own adventure. But it is my journey I must focus on: my journey to find them. I have not stopped searching for them nor will I ever stop. I will find my sons.

The moment I arrived in Midgard, I began my search. After defying the will of the gods and escaping Asgard across Bifrost, the Rainbow Bridge, I found myself in the midst of a beautiful forest, green and alive. It did not seem real to me because in many ways, the forest held more beauty than those in Asgard. Many hours I had spent convincing myself that I was in Alfheim, world of the elves, for surely only in Alfheim could there be forests as lovely as those. However, Bifrost only connects Asgard to Midgard and that is where I stood.

My heart was happy. After so long trapped in Asgard within a city of stone and structure, I had finally returned to the wild. To the forest. I could feel the wolf in me returning. But is this where Sköll and Hati arrived when they were banished?

PETER CURSON

  I spent many a day roaming through the forest, seemingly endless, for besides the occasional clearing or lake, all I could find was more trees. Yet I kept moving. I always kept moving. And, of course, I was shifted. There was no reason not to; there are no Æsir on Midgard, and the humans are powerless to stop me. Not only did I wander in wolf form for my own protection, I crossed land far quicker and with less energy. But most of all, it was for my own enjoyment. I could smell all the scents in their abundance and hear the critters and the wind between the trees. I could feel the soil beneath my paws and sink my fangs into my food, tasting blood as it washed over my tongue and flesh as it filled my belly. This is what I am meant to be. I am a wolf. This who I am.
  The forests of that land where I began my journey are so green, bountiful with plants and trees. Even where dead and dying trees stood, vibrant green moss covered them from root to branch. If not for the brilliant blue sky above the towering canopies, I did not think there was any other color on Midgard than its many shades of green and brown.
  The plants and trees and tall grasses drank from the many streams and creeks and bathed in a warm but intermittent sun. It was spring then, which meant rain. Lots of it. The sun could shine in the morning and a torrent could follow in the afternoon. But the rain, as dreadful and cold as it was, brought further life to the forest, enhancing the smells and scents of all things. I have found no smell nicer on Midgard than the forest after it rains.
  And the animals were rampant! I could catch a bear every day if I wished, and often I did. Squirrels were abundant even for the high number of coyotes constantly chasing them amidst the undergrowth. I came across the occasional deer and the even rarer rabbit. And of course the many birds of the air, from the smallest birds chasing each other between the trees to the wide-eyed owls observing from their perches to the

LEGEND OF FENRIR

large eagles circling overhead.
  I loved those lands. But it did not take long until I realized I had no plan. How could I find my sons in such a large world? They could be anywhere on Midgard and I have found no track or scent of them. So, as I learned during my time in Asgard, I changed my process and my way of thinking. No, my sons could not be anywhere. They would not settle in a desert, nor would they settle on a desolate mountain peak. They would find a place that is safe and with plenty of prey. They would need water and they would need shelter. Where I find that, I may find my sons.
  I decided to travel west and only west in hopes of exiting the forest. When I did days later, I stood atop a plateau and before me ran a rather large river winding its way through the land. I could smell some salt in the water, which told me a sea or ocean was near. Beyond the river, the land rose and then fell again into the distance where mountains rose tall and proud. Further yet, forests covered the mountains like blankets. Surely wolves and bears and deer call those mountains home. They are high and can see far and wide in all directions. If I was not looking for Sköll and Hati, I would make those mountains my home. It was as good a place to start as any.
  For the day after crossing the river, I trudged through more forest land, climbing the large hill until the strong smell of smelly fish met me. I followed the scent, which brought me to a small inlet that sat surrounded by mountains——the beginnings of a long mountain range rising to the north.
  In the water, I saw seals playing in the steady waters, oftentimes poking their heads out of the water to feel the nice breeze and then diving back in. Families of brown-colored geese flocked to the inlet, flopping into the water to enjoy a swim. The young goslings, newly born, pipped and squeaked with delight but their parents made the most ungodly noises I have ever heard: the first and only downfall of that land.

PETER CURSON

With great pleasure, I swam across the chilled water to the foot of the mountains and followed the inlet west, marveling at the tree-covered mountains around me. Some mountains were small, too large to be called hills, and some were as large as those in Asgard. Soon, the inlet separated into two arms: one continuing to lead west and one coming from the north. The mountains followed both paths, but fell to the ground west and rose higher in the sky north. This was the first fork in my journey and I stood at a loss. How did the adventurers of old decide which path to next explore when met with a crossroad? But more importantly, where would Sköll and Hati have gone?

It was in this moment when despair seeped through. I imagined myself taking one path and having my sons down the other. And then it got worse. What if they were not in the west at all, but east from where I began? All decisions from here could prove useless, all my effort for naught, and my searching in vain.

Despair gripped my heart, but only for a moment did I let it win. Only for one moment and then I forced it from myself for it would do nothing but hinder me further. I would allow nothing to keep me from finding my sons, and if Sköll and Hati indeed traveled east when I traveled west, I would take heart knowing I would meet them on the other side of the world. Thus, I had to press on trusting in my instincts as I always have.

I looked at the paths before me again. The wind brought the smell of salt and fish from the west—an ocean breeze. But I could sense wildlife in the north and the security of the mountains. It would not make much sense for a wolf to travel to the ocean, for what prey is there along the shoreline? The bears and coyotes of this land hunt small critters, and those small critters take refuge within the forest. Where prey hides, predators stalk. And where predators stalk is where my

LEGEND OF FENRIR

sons would thrive for now they stand at the zenith of the food chain. The route north appears to be the logical option, but I would not make a move until I was sure I came to the same conclusion my sons would have. They are young, after all, and have never been in the wild on their own. It may take them longer to arrive to the same conclusions I do. Yet, they are wolves and their instinct to survive will not fail them.

    I remember it was nearing sundown and I sat upon a rocky beach when my ears perked and I felt an instinct I had not felt since before I arrived in Midgard: presence. I sat still a moment longer and then I heard it. Talking. The humans. The sound came from the north upon the water, just around the bend. I silently made my way off the beach and hid myself within the tree line. I was confident that the humans posed no threat but what good would it do to reveal my existence to them? Besides, my curiosity could not be quelled. Who were these humans? What were they like? How did they live? All questions I wanted answered. After a few minutes of anticipation, I saw them.

    Eight human men sat in long, skinny boats, two to each, which they propelled with wooden paddles. They transported hunted animals in their boats and carried with them bows enough for each man with many arrows. They had large nets full of fish with them as well—their primary means of food. Their skin was dark, darker than the Norsemen, but I did recognize their look for there were many men sharing their complexion within the ranks of the Einherjar. But were these men warriors or just hunters and fishers?

    Their clothing was simple and there was not one sword among them. A couple spears I saw but with heads of stone or bone. Did they not forge metal? Regardless, their spoils for the day were plenty. They are hunters, and good hunters at that, and I would not underestimate them. One thing was made clear to me here: I was not in the land of the

PETER CURSON

Norsemen.
    They paddled down the inlet speaking in a language I have never heard. They seemed calm. Collected. Sort of at peace. My heart warmed at the thought. It is something I have never known. Even before I was captured by the Æsir, my family still lived in Asgard. There was never a true peace for us; conflict of some kind always haunted us. It did not appear so for these men.
    When they reached the fork in the water, they turned down the path leading west. It was near the end of the day and their boats were full of food. They were returning home. The humans, at least the people from which these men came, must then make their home by the ocean, not in the northern mountains. My curiosity drew me west, but I had to think of my sons. Would they take the safe route north or scout out the inhabitants of the land? As their father, I would have them take the safe route. But as their father, I knew that with their thick skulls, they would think themselves the alpha-predators of not just the wildlife, but all of Midgard. And so they will have gone west. And so did I.

    Their land is breathtaking. The inlet kept running west with the mountains on its northern shore and the forest on its southern until at last the inlet hit a peninsula alive with trees, thousands upon thousands of them on this large piece of land, some growing hundreds of feet in the air. A utopia it was, surrounded by water on all sides save for the small area connecting to the mainland. Now that is a place to make a home. And the humans did.
    On the eastern shore of the peninsula stood a village. Boats were moored there on the shore with many houses built of wood between the water and trees. In the center of this village was a longhouse that I surmise could shelter one hundred people. But from what I could scout, there were close to

LEGEND OF FENRIR

three hundred people in this simple village.

For two days and nights I watched them from the southern shore of the peninsula. Many of the men left on foot and boat with their spears and bows to hunt while lots of the women ventured into the forest to gather. But there were always men guarding their village with spears and bows within arm's reach. Warriors. And there would only be one reason for that: another people must be nearby. A hostile people. And I soon turned out to be correct.

On the third day, they came from the south at sun's first light. I heard them some short way from my position and I sulked back into the brush, having to shift back to my normal, human-like self in order to fully conceal myself even in the tallest of bushes. They came quickly and silently. To each man was at least one weapon: spear, bow, spade, or stone hammer. However, they outnumbered the village guards five to one. It was not an army, but a raiding party, meant to attack while most of the men were away. It would be a slaughter. But it was not my fight and therefore not my concern. So I let them pass me without a sound and they were off northward to the village.

I sat in silence for a short while, shuffling and itching. Very rarely can I not sit still. My instincts called me to action, but for what purpose? Though I know with full confidence I could take on the raiding party single-handedly, why would I risk any harm to myself for humans who have done nothing for me. For all I know, the people on the water could have raided these peoples' villages the day before. Yet, it troubled me that I did not know what the raiding party meant to do. Did they mean to take food and tools or did they mean to kill the people—the women and children. Nay, I could not stand idly by while children might face death. I jumped up, shifted, and ran after the raiding party hoping I was not too late.

I was.

PETER CURSON

As I neared the forest's edge by the village, I could already hear the cries of war and the screams of fear. But I would not reveal myself as a wolf to those whom I do not know. I shifted back, sprinting as fast as my two legs could go and broke through the tree line, immediately attacking five of their archers. They were no match for one of the Jötnar. I took the fifth archer to the ground and when I looked up, I saw that all but one of the village's guard were dead. The last man, holding a spear with a broken shaft, stood in front of a group of children protecting them at all costs from the several remaining raiders. The terror in those children's eyes brought forth increased vigor from within me and I charged at the raiders.

Only a few came at me, the rest thinking I would be easily killed. The first man thrust a spear towards my head. I grabbed it by the shaft, pulled him in, and twisted his neck completely around. The other two advanced upon me. I cast the stone spear into one of their chests and to the other I twisted his arm and smashed his face into the ground, crushing his skull beneath my palm. The remaining raiders, now with visible hesitation, charged me all at once. I defeated them without so much as a scratch, leaving only one alive. Bleeding from his nose and mouth, I held him by the shirt and looked deep into his weakened eyes.

"Do not come back," I said to him. I knew he did not speak my words but I could see in his eyes he knew my meaning. I cast him to the side with strength beyond any human comprehension and repeated my command. "Do not come back." He scampered away as though he was running from a hundred angry bears.

The villagers gathered around me and murmured amongst themselves. The young children were frightened, the older ones awed and curious. I could not understand them. Perhaps they were speaking of my act of rescue, or of my fighting ability, or even of my skin's complexion. But my focus

LEGEND OF FENRIR

was on the last of their warriors. At first, he was hesitant, which was to be expected because I too was a warrior to be reckoned with. But when he saw that I showed no hostility and meant them no harm, he dropped his broken spear and approached me with his hands held out in thanks. I took them and he gripped mine tightly and spoke some words. He seemed humble. But above all, I could sense his gratitude.

The villagers sat me in their longhouse, persistent on thanking me for rescuing them and saving their village. A few of the older women in the group brought me a large salmon which was cooked on a plank of wood. The salmon itself was quite different from the fish my brother Jormungand used to catch back home. It was incredible. The taste of the fish and the way in which it was smoked and prepared is something I will never forget—I have always wanted to go back and eat their salmon again.

As I sat in silence with the humans while they watched me, I could not help but think back to the days when Jor, my sister Hél, and I would be out in the wilderness. Jor would walk straight for the lake and there he would shift. I can see him now, one second standing larger and just taller than me and the next, his body rising high into the air as he morphed into a giant sea serpent the likes of which no human mythical tales tell of. He would tip over and come crashing down into the strait by our home, sending waves as large as trees crashing all around him. While he fished, I would continue on to the forest and there I would hunt. Then we would put our bounties together and make for home for a big feast.

That meal with the humans was no feast, at least not for my large stomach, but I appreciated the gesture nonetheless, as well as the opportunity to taste new foods prepared differently to what I had ever seen.

When the rest of their people returned from the hunts and the forest, the warrior explained to them what took place.

PETER CURSON

I wish I knew what he said, and what they said in reply. Some seemed skeptical of me, glancing at me with unsure eyes as if they had let a racoon into their home, waiting for me to run amuck and tear everything apart. Some men seemed overjoyed that I came and killed the raid party. Why would they not? If not for me, the village would not have been here to return to. They all knew that, I have no doubts about it. But that act alone does not grant total trust, especially when half of your warriors have been killed. It took a long discussion but they eventually accepted me into their village and, from what I could tell, thanked me profusely.

    I spent two weeks with the humans. It was best to keep this tribe as an ally while I search for my sons because I would not have been able to make any progress sneaking past them. I joined the hunters when they went into the northern mountains, most times sticking with the group and wincing as I limited myself to bow and arrow, but sometimes I would move off on my own, shift, and catch many animals, sticking them with arrows after catching them. Yet in all the time I was out there in the mountains, I found no sign of Sköll and Hati.
    In the times we were not hunting, I spent my time mostly with two men whose names were Matunaagd and Megedagik. It was clear to me they were the strongest and most skilled warriors in their tribe, and they were excellent hunters. But what surprised me was that they were very patient and quick to smile. They would sit with me and try to teach me their language, which was no easy thing. First, I learned their names and they learned mine and when I taught them to pronounce Fenrir, they never stopped saying it! And they always said it with a smile. Such a simple thing but something I have never forgotten.
    I then learned the name for their people: Sko-ko-mish, and the name for their village: Xwayxway. Beyond that, I could

LEGEND OF FENRIR

not grasp their language. We each would speak in our own tongues, but I do not think anything stuck in their minds. Perhaps given time, but I did not have time. It had been two weeks and without sign of my sons, I could only surmise they moved on from this land—if they were ever here at all.

One night, I sat with Matunaagd and Megedagik around the fire as the sky turned from blue to black. I knew that it was to be my last night there and that I would depart their lands once everyone went to sleep. It pained me to even come to that decision because they treated me as one of their own. They deserved an explanation but I could not give one. And they deserved a proper farewell. Yet I could not bring myself to tell them; it was easier this way. I did, however, have one thing left to ask.

I broke the silence of night knowing they would not understand my words, but I told them, "I am looking for my sons." And when their inevitable faces of confusion shown in the firelight, I brought my hands atop my head and shaped them like a wolf's ears and I howled. Then I held up two fingers, counting them, and stretched out my arms wide, meaning big.

"*U'ligan*," they both said. But they shook their heads and brought in their hands, meaning small, then moved them around as though there were many, not just two. They have not seen my sons. It saddened me for I allowed my heart to hope. Hope that they knew where my sons were, or hope that they had seen them and could point me in the right direction. But it was not a surprise. There was nothing to be done but continue my search.

My two friends went to sleep but I stayed by the fire a while longer. I made friends. And it made me think of Týr and Balder. Despite being of the High-Æsir, they looked past my Jötunn heritage and saw me as me. As Fenrir. Much to the dislike of their comrades, the most of which Thor, they did

PETER CURSON

not want to further the conflict we faced. They still saw the Jötnar as their enemies, but they knew that race and war were not to be looked at as black and white, that one race or one side was entirely good or entirely evil. They indeed stand against my race in war, but that does not make every individual Jötunn their enemy, just as Týr and Balder were not my enemies. They were friends among enemies. And I found myself missing them. I wondered if I would miss Matunaagd and Megedagik too. And I surely have. Even to this day, I think about going back to Xwayxway. Life was so simple there and it reminded me of my time in Asgard before any of this happened, before I was captured by the Æsir, before my siblings and I were unjustly punished, before… when I was happy.

    Alas, I stood and turned to leave Xwayxway but as I did, my ear twitched and an arrow streamed past my eyes and two more landed at my feet. From the south came many warriors from the other tribe. This time it was no raiding party. This was their entire fighting strength. I shouted as loud as I could, "Attack! Attack!" The men scrambled out of their homes but the enemy was already upon us. I took on as many as I could, keeping them from the center of the village but many slipped past. Matunaagd and Megedagik found me within moments and the three of us fought side-by-side. The Sko-ko-mish warriors took up arms and fought back with stout hearts while the women grabbed the children and scattered into the safety of the forest. But we were outnumbered and they came to kill. And it was in the exact moment that I realized we could not gain victory when Matunaagd was pierced by an arrow, but still he raged on with such fury and fire even the gods would fear him. Yet still, his knees shook and a group of warriors pressed against him. The Sko-ko-mish around me dwindled. Hope faded. There was only one thing left to do. I threw aside my foe and sprinted towards the oncoming men, leaping high into the air, and shifted, crashing

LEGEND OF FENRIR

upon them with my jaws open wide. The noise of war silenced and all that filled the air were my snarls and the ripping of flesh from bone until naught was left but the corpses of our enemy and one man left standing: the same man who I let escape two weeks before. I shifted back and when I approached, I did not hesitate in killing him and watched as the fear and regret faded from his eyes as his blood poured out from his severed head.

When I turned back to face the Sko-ko-mish, they backed away in fear. All except Megedagik, who helped Matunaagd over to me. He clasped me on the shoulder and said one word to me before he died, one word in my own language. And he said it perfectly.

I stayed a while longer that night to help Megedagik dig Matunaagd's grave. No words were spoken between us but I could sense no fear from him. I am sure he was pained from all the questions he wanted to ask with no way of asking them. When all was finished, Megedagik knew I had to leave and so he embraced me and parted from me with a smile before returning to his people.

I stood there where Matunaagd now rests and before I left, I repeated his word. "Friend."

ᛏᚹᛟ

TWO

I spent the next part of that spring traveling north through the mountains, which seemed to never end. To the west flowed a strait full of tiny islands dotting the water between the land I searched and another land across. The strait followed the mountains, which were separated by many sounds and inlets, all the way north until the western land ended and all that remained west was the ocean. I traveled over the mountain peaks covered with snow and ice, careful to watch my steps for the snowpack was weakening with each passing day and every so often I would see a cornice of snow overhanging a cliff give way and tumble down the slopes below. The winter must have been a cold one indeed if the mountains were covered as they were.

Spring was great, full of everything needed for long travels: sun, a cool breeze, and crisp air. The animals were also out in great numbers, not yet culled by their predators. However, the rain atop these mountains turned the snow heavy and when the sun shone next, its rays froze the wet, heavy snow

LEGEND OF FENRIR

into sheets of crunchy ice. If not for my large paws, the conditions would have forced me to wait until warmer days. Regardless, my travels were sound and the landscape—the mountains, the ocean, and the deep green forests—was my only comfort as I searched to no avail for any sign of my sons. Despite the lovely spring, I longed for winter in those days. Nothing compares to the season's first snow. How quiet and blissful it is, something that would comfort my gloomy heart. The soft powdery snow would have been in much more delight. But the lack of food would have been a great hinderance, especially up upon the mountain peaks. Alas, spring was the right time to leave for it gave me the most amount of days to travel as the days grew longer.

I did not encounter any more humans for quite some time. Nor did I encounter Sköll or Hati. Traversing the mountain peaks was not difficult while I was shifted in my wolf form, and when I reached each peak, I would let out a loud and clear howl—a call to my sons—in hopes they would hear me. I waited for their responses. None ever came.

The same day I left the strait behind and found the ocean ahead, I stumbled upon more humans while traversing a valley between mountains. They had finished hunting for the day but were returning empty-handed. I followed them back to their village. It was smaller than Xwayxway but they lived very similarly. An idea formed in my mind.

I spent the remaining daylit hours scouring the forest, finally finding and catching a deer. I brought it close to their village in my jaws but then shifted back to my normal form and carried it over my shoulder into their village as an offer of peace. As expected, they were hesitant about an outsider with appearance they had never seen before. But I did not come to stay.

"*U'ligan*," I said, repeating the word with my arms

PETER CURSON

open wide and counting two on my fingers, but they did not understand my meaning, for a group of men, hunters by the looks of them, grabbed their bows. Perhaps they thought I was trying to warn them of two big wolves. One way or the other, if they encountered my sons, they would have known what I was trying to say. So I gave them the deer and left their village, continuing north through the mountains.

When spring neared its end and summer embraced the northern lands, I had left the forests and forest covered mountains behind. In their place came a vast tundra. Mountains still rose but they were rocky and barren with only few trees to cover them. Vibrant green shrubs and grass painted the fields between the barren mountains and in some fields, flowers bloomed with bright colors celebrating a winter survived and a summer retuned. I was far north indeed. But I still did not find the Norsemen. And that was where I made my first mistake on Midgard.

The barren landscape filled me with a sense of solitude and seclusion so I deemed it fine to wander in my wolf form to cover more ground in each day. It was faster that way, after all. One day, however, I was beset by a herd of oversized reindeer; a hunting party was at their backs. The humans looked similar to the Sko-ko-mish and they turned tail at the sight of me screaming the same word repeatedly: "*Amarok*!"

I did not think much of it at the time and continued my journey. The land began to curve westward and I decided to follow it since the humans fled eastward. But one night, I was startled awake by the sound of heavy footsteps approaching from all around me. Several dozens of men advanced from all sides with all sorts of weapons in hand. They left me no option. I left that battleground with negligible cuts and scratches, leaving be any who wished retreat.

Do all humans act the same? If so, they are all foolish.

LEGEND OF FENRIR

The man I let escape back in Xwayxway did not take it as an act of grace and returned only to be slaughtered. These humans saw me, a monster to their eyes, and even though I did not show them a lick of hostility, they came after me with intent to kill. If they stayed away, none of them would have ever seen me again. Now their people have lost many of their men and most of their warriors. But I did not think much of it. What concern was it to me?

    I decided best to continue my journey for I was certain word of the *Amarok* would spread and I had no want to be attacked in my sleep again. That very night, in the starlit sky above appeared a strange thing: a string of glowing lights slithering through the sky in many shades of green and pink. For a moment, I believed it to be Bifrost, the Rainbow Bridge that connects Asgard and Midgard. But it was not so. The lights only shone at night. Midgard does hold some magic after all.

    The skyward lights brought a comfort that I cannot explain. Some nights, I sat for many hours watching them wave back and forth in their hypnotic dance. Glimmers would fade away as a shadow and then reappear with more intensity than before, rejoining the endless string of lights winding their way to the edge of night. I was so mesmerized. That comfort was so powerful I decided to continue my travels at night. I would sleep during the day, rising near dusk to catch a bear or one of those large reindeer, or a moose if I was lucky, and spend my night continuing north and west, following the beautiful lights in the sky.

    I took care to avoid the numerous villages along the way. Yet I could not prevent all human contact. I stumbled upon a couple hunting parties, or they stumbled upon me, and they fled shouting that same word, "*Amarok*." I wonder if that is their word for wolf. Or monster. Or monster wolf. Regardless, no more warriors came against me. Perhaps they heard of what I did to the last group of people who tried ambushing

PETER CURSON

me.

    Alas, I ventured so far to the west that I met the ocean once more. Even though it was now summer, the mountains still clung to their snow and ice, which revealed more of the ocean's shoreline. The tide was extremely far out, perhaps from all the glaciers remaining intact. And though the ocean stretched far, I saw two islands poking out of the water. Behind them, on the far horizon, my eyes could barely pick out something breaking the uniformity of the water—what I believed to be more mountains. West. I have to keep moving west. I have told myself over and over again that I picked a direction and I must keep to it. For if I change my direction, I may be moving away from my sons. They may be across the ocean. And if they are, I could spend a hundred years on this side of the ocean searching in vain. Nay, I must keep moving west until I can no longer move west or I arrive back where I began.

    Though the islands were far off, as humans are concerned, I could manage the swim in wolf form, and possibly the mountains thereafter, but I would not risk it in these arctic waters. Further yet, there was no promise of food on the other side even if I could make it. Adequate preparations were in order so that I could take food with me enough to last a day after I arrive at those western mountains, which meant I was going to need a boat.

    A village stood not too far back from the western shore so I ventured back and under the light of the moon and sky-lights and in my normal form, I infiltrated the village like a thief in the dark, taking one of their boats. When I was sure I left without anyone noticing, I carried it a short way down the shoreline and waited until morning. At first light, I hunted myself a deer for breakfast and managed to catch a few white foxes that I would take along to sustain me until I could find more prey in the far-off mountains.

LEGEND OF FENRIR

Not wishing to waste anymore daylight than I needed, I pushed off the shore and paddled towards the two islands. The ocean current was quite calm within this strait but the distance I needed to travel was so far that even my Jötunn arms began to tire. Each stroke took a toll on my muscles, which were unfamiliar with paddling to begin with. The weariness not only attacked my body, but also my mind.

When my arms tired to the point of hurting, my resolve diminished just enough to let slip unfavorable thoughts. With each painful stroke, the same question ran through my mind: did Sköll and Hati even come this way? They would have had to steal a boat as well. What if they did not plan and take extra food? What if they searched those mountains until starvation forced their bodies to eternal rest?

That last thought tore my mind away from the downward spiral of doubt. Instead, it drove me forward and I paddled with more purpose than when I started. The aching in my arms increased but it fueled me. I focused on the pain because it was through that pain that I would find my sons. And I would endure this pain for a hundred years before I would allow myself to succumb to any such sinister thoughts. So I forced the thought from my mind and stared at that horizon with unshakeable determination.

Before I knew it, I made it to the first island at sundown. It was barren, surrounded by near vertical cliffs with a plateau as its peak—like the tip of a mountain rising from the water. Beyond it rose the second, larger island, also with steep cliffs but with an actual landscape atop sharp-sloping hills. I continued to the larger island, found a beach shallow enough to moor upon. After the simple climb up the hill, I spent a while sitting upon the edge of a cliff eating one of my foxes and gazing at the perfectly cloudless sky.

It was a wonderful night even though I had no one to

PETER CURSON

share it with. I like being alone. No trouble comes from solitude. Though some cannot bear the loneliness, it does not deter me. I do not need others. Indeed, I miss my wife and sons more than anything in any of the Nine Worlds, but I have learned to be content with myself and myself alone. Some wolves need a pack. Some are better off lone.

I made it to the western mountains the next night after another grueling day of paddling. With weak and shaking arms, I ate my last fox. Though I was famished—foxes as small as they are barely fill my stomach—I decided to find a safe place to sleep and hunt in the morning. As it turned out, the mountains were only small along the coastline but they were all barren in this far northern region. It took some time but I did indeed find a couple of odd-looking deer to satisfy my hunger, then went at once to traverse the mountains.

I felt a certain homeliness within these mountains despite not having any trees. I could not place why at first. It was more of an underlying feeling. An instinctual one. It did not take too long to find out why.

There were predators everywhere.

The deer were in plenty and a type of elk new to my eyes was in even greater number, which allowed for numerous predators even in this cold, barren environment. The first I saw was a burly bear with light brown fur to match the barren dirt. They proved to be more ferocious than those from the lands north of Xwayxway. Whereas those bears fished for salmon in the many streams and rivers that slithered through their territories, these bears were not so fortunate and had to resort to what food they could stumble upon. Sometimes this meant trapping a deer, or fellow predator if they could, but mostly they ate what plants they could find. I had never seen such a big and fearsome predator eat so much grass and shoots before. It was quite the sight indeed.

LEGEND OF FENRIR

The next predators I saw stood off against one another and I took care not to alert them to my presence because of how fascinating they were! One stood just shorter than a bear while the other stood just shorter than both, but their bodies were just as long—if you do not include their tails. One of the animals, the smaller of the two stood over an elk carcass with blood staining its fangs and whiskers. Its fur was a vivid light-yellow but what drew my eyes to it was all the black spots covering its body from its nose all the way to the tip of its slightly curved tail. The other, larger predator slowly advanced towards the fallen elk. It shared the same body type as the spotted animal down to its facial structure. This animal was not yellow, but orange and was not dotted by black spots but lined with black stripes from its nose to the tip of its tail. It roared in intimidation but it only enticed the spotted animal and it charged.

The battle over the elk was extreme and violent, to say the least. The spotted animal was quicker both in footstep and attack, swiping rapidly and trying to climb on top of his opponent, but the striped animal was all the stronger and would not budge in his attack. They became entangled. Watching them brought forth a strong urge in me to fight but I could not tear myself from watching these two vicious, yet exquisite animals. Finally, the striped animal forced itself upon his foe and clamped its fangs hard into the spotted animals neck. A killing blow. He held his fangs there for a while longer, savoring the blood in his mouth while it was still warm. A well-fought victory. I had half a mind to move in and kill it and take all three for my own, but I felt a respect for the predator and allowed it to keep its prizes that day. Yet from that day onward, I could never bring myself to hunt one of the orange and black animals, only the bears and the spotted ones. They certainly are my favorite animal here on Midgard.

When I finally arrived at the western face of the

PETER CURSON

mountains, I saw before me a vast tundra interspersed with small lakes that stretched into the distance where another mountain range formed once again. Why does Midgard have to have so many mountains? Alas, one leg of my journey led to the next. The question for me then was: how long will this leg be?

Winter came. And it was unlike any winter I had ever faced in Asgard. The dark disease of cold and snow wiped out all the living, covering everything green and growing in a sheet of frozen death. Darkness fell, the days becoming shorter than I had ever seen them—at the heart of winter, the sun never even rose above the horizon, brightening the sky for only a pittance of time just to show the world it still existed. And the wind blew for months at a time. Even as a wolf I was cold. The frigid gales blew the snow like shards of glass through the air and covered absolutely everything in sight. The only time I had seen such an environment was when I laid eyes on Niflheim, the world of everlasting ice.

Thus, I spent most of that winter huddled within a snow cave I dug; there was no traveling in such a harsh winter. I spent many of those days regretting my choice of direction. After crossing the ocean near the end of summer and traversing the predator-filled mountains, a wide plain stretched west with mountains skirting its southern side. It was a simple path to take west. It was so easy with suitable terrain, plenty of animals, and no humans, that I decided to continue on through the autumn months when the temperature dropped and the darkness grew. Before I knew it, the plains were covered in snow up to my belly in my wolf form. I could not brave the blizzards and the cold all the while trudging through dozens of feet of snow. If only I had traveled south for some length of time and then west, I might have been able to travel with relative ease. Or maybe all of Midgard freezes over like this in

LEGEND OF FENRIR

the winter. The snow did remain on the mountain peaks in some places even into the summer back on the land where I began my journey. In any regard, I was stuck in that snow ridden land.

When the weather took a breath between blizzards, I scurried about the frozen domain, finding the dens where bears had hidden themselves for their winter sleep. I would kill them and carry them back, fattening myself and lining the floor of my cave with their furs for the long days ahead. And long they were. Most nights were filled with the wailing of the wind while clouds blanketed the sky.

I missed the warmer seasons and yearned for spring's return. Nay, I yearned for a mild winter. A blissful snowfall and a chilled breeze. Snow deep enough to pad the ground for my paws that I did not have to dig through with each step. A temperature cold enough to see my breath but not enough to keep me shivering. A mild winter. Not a wintry nightmare.

But every now and then, when the hiding sun took back its light like a jealous dwarf not wishing to share his gold, and it left the cold of night in its wake, the clouds would clear revealing the sky-lights renewed with such brilliant intensity and radiance. They gave me the will to endure that winter. And they gave me hope for my journey ahead.

I left my cave when the temperature started to rise, awakening from the world's dark slumber. It rose slowly at first, still below the point of freezing, but I would not waste any more time before resuming the search for my sons once more. My trek continued ever on west. The mountains rose in the south, but as the land stretched north, it plateaued into great plains covered in snow and ice. I kept to the foot of the mountains for ease of travel and for ease of hunting. I started to see the wildlife crawling up from the depths of the frozen ground, and it made my heart content. Life was returning to

PETER CURSON

the world, roaming wild as all creatures should. The bears, however, mostly still slept, which made for easy pickings. I traveled further and further as winter fully passed and spring brought its sun and its eventual warmth, gradually taking the snow from the land.

I stumbled upon numerous more tribes of humans along the way. The first I saw in that spring, I made contact with in hopes they had seen my sons in their lands. This tribe was nomadic, living in tents by night and moving by wooden sled during the day. As always, I brought a deer as a gift. These nomads looked different than the Sko-ko-mish and spoke a very different language. Furthermore, they were more advanced.

They had domesticated reindeer with saddles on them that they used to ride like horses across the wintry plains. And what was more, they had steel. Spearheads, arrowheads, and tools. These people, however, did not seem curious of my complexion nor my height. I asked my question and with the same unhelpful response, I left. They seemed curiously reluctant to even listen to what I had to say. And when I turned my back, they attacked.

I shifted.

They surrendered immediately.

What drove them to attack a man who did not threaten them, even leaving a deer as a gift, I could not tell. I wish I could have asked them. Perhaps I had entered into a land where war was commonplace. Maybe their way of thinking was more primitive, having a pronounced fight instinct in them. Anyone who could be a threat, especially one that knew of their whereabouts, was better off dead. Regardless of their reasoning, I left all who surrendered alive; I was not in the habit of killing unnecessarily. And when I left, still in wolf form, I heard the people whisper a strange word, "*Vuko-dlak.*" And that word traveled before me across the land, for when

LEGEND OF FENRIR

any other human by chance saw me, they fled in terror screaming that same word. All was well, it made my travels easier.

By mid-spring, I came to more populated regions. The nomadic tribes became fewer in number and in their place were peoples who settled in built-up villages. But what I saw there, where I had not seen thus far, were the beginnings of civilization. The villages had houses of wood, there was a forgery in the larger villages, and they were connected by roads. Iron and bronze were common for tools and weaponry. And when the humans did not barter for items, they used silver and sometimes gold coins. And to my delight, I saw traveling merchants frequent these villages on horses. I no longer had to hide in the shadows. All I needed to do was seize a horse and cart and travel under the guise of a merchant. There would be no better way to talk to the villagers of the lands in hopes of hearing rumors of my sons.

And so that is what I did. I traveled from village to village as the days grew longer and longer once more. It was quite the change switching roles as a hunter in lands without civilization to become a merchant moving from town to town bartering and haggling with people. It altered my instincts. Survival was still foremost in my mind, but of a less-baser caliber. Survival did not mean hunting prey and avoiding or fighting human predators. Survival meant knowing who to trust, who to avoid, and who to exploit. It meant examining people and judging whether they would attack you for your goods. One thing, however, did not change: always, always watching your back.

But I found myself surviving all the same. I always got my way when interacting with the humans seeking information, food, or trading. Perhaps it was my confidence in my fighting ability that kept me from harm. Backing down from the humans never entered my mind and that transferred into my haggles. I engaged in many bouts of words but knew that

PETER CURSON

I could say and do whatever I wanted for what could the humans do but put up a losing fight? And just as that stubbornness resulted in many altercations, it led me out of them the victor all the same.

Dealing with the humans like this on a daily basis was a struggle and one of the greatest irritants I have ever had to face. But it brought me out of a deep despondency, brought forth by many long months in isolation. A wolf I am. A lone wolf. But a Jötunn I am first, and like the humans, we need interaction to keep sane. Maybe not to the same degree; there are many humans not right in their heads. But all the same, the interactions, the conversations, the occasional sharing of laughter and stories with a stranger made a world of difference.

I continued my travels throughout that land steadily but with purpose, never staying in one place longer than needed. Just as I was getting a grasp of one language, I had moved too far west where there was a new people and a new language. But one thing was consistent: no one knew a thing about my sons. Maybe I got it all wrong, maybe they are not roaming Midgard as wolves, but as "humans." Blending in. Surviving as I am now. It did not settle in my mind, however. They are not paranoid nor are they fearful. They would not hide their wolf-forms out of fear. The only reason they would become one with the humans was for a clear benefit to their life here on Midgard. Perhaps they did not arrive in Midgard in the middle of the wild like I did. Instead, they could have arrived on the outskirts of a large, rich town in which they could become men of power. Hah. Lord Sköll and Lord Hati. An entertaining thought, but if proven true, would make the search unfathomably more difficult.

Despite this concern, I pressed westward. The northern lands stretch far indeed, but their wondrous landscapes cannot be matched, save perhaps by those in Jötunheim. My

LEGEND OF FENRIR

mother has told me many stories of that land. The dark forests, the menacing mountains, the fell beasts roaming the lands. They filled me with a sense of excitement along with my feelings of yearning for my homeland. Hunting in Midgard and Asgard rarely proved a challenge, offering but a pittance of thrill. But in Jötunheim, the beasts prove as tall and menacing as me. The danger, the uncertainty. How fun it would be!

One day, when spring neared its end, I traveled to a large town on the shore of a great sea. Merchants gathered there from all sorts of places. It was quite something to see so many foreigners interacting with one another without sharing a common language. That place, which acted as an entire marketplace, was easily the largest town I had yet visited on Midgard. It was called Turgu. I spent a couple of days meeting different merchants, some from the east whose people I have already met, and many from the south. The variety of cultures from the south and the differences between them are astounding. Everything from how they converse and barter to how they wear their clothes and how they eat. I found my curiosity at its peak the entire time in that city, but could do nothing to satisfy it. Regardless, if I could one day travel south, I would like to see what their people have to offer.

On my third day in Turgu, while three different men from three different peoples were haggling with me for a bear that I had caught, I heard from down the road something that I thought I recognized. It was my language. I quickly grabbed the silver from a dark-skinned man's hand and pushed my way down the road until I found the only man who I could understand. He was large, from his blonde head to toe, and he sold iron tools from hammers to axes.

"Hello," I said in our tongue.

"Ah, another Norseman in these parts. Always a pleasure. What are you looking for?" My heart quickened; he was one of the Norsemen! Questions ran through my mind one after the other. Was I near their lands? Or has he traveled far from them? Does he know of my sons? Finally, I can ask someone properly.

"Actually, I am looking for information," I said. "Have you heard any rumors about two large wolves, black as night?"

"Not two wolves, but I have heard rumors about the *Vuko-dlak*, as these people east of the sea name it: a large wolf, the size of a bear tenfold, that wanders the lands east of here. In the south, they name it *Werwulf* and our people name it *Var-ulv*, but it is in fact a man who can shift into the monstrous wolf—if you believe in such monsters."

"Do you believe in them?"

"I believe what I can see," he replied. "But there have been increasing amount of talk about monsters back in Svea-land."

"Two wolves?"

"Nay, one dragon and one sea serpent. But if you are looking for anything more, you will have better luck asking the folk in Birca."

"Where is Birca?"

He stopped and looked at me, confused. "How do you not know where Birca is?"

"You mistake my meaning," I said, thinking quickly. "Where is Birca from here? In which direction must I travel? I traveled south from our lands many summers ago and have never been to these parts."

His look of confusion subsided a little, but I could see doubt still gnawed at his mind. "West, across the sea. You will need to fetch a ride on a boat. But how—"

"Thank you," I interjected and took my leave quickly. I took my cart and made straight for the boats. I could not calm myself, for even though he did not mention anything

LEGEND OF FENRIR

about Sköll and Hati, he mentioned a sea serpent, and I know of only one of those in Midgard.

THREE

Birca, the trading capital of the North. I thought Turgu was a large marketplace, but this city, situated on an island within the mainland, was simply alive with people. Many rivers flow into the heart of Svealand from the eastern shores creating many islands surrounded by land. Being so close to the sea with many waterways to and from this island amongst islands, it is a prime choice in becoming an established trading capital. It is beautiful in every aspect of the word. The island on which Birca stands is covered in trees with grassy fields filling in the gaps, with rocky terrain adding some flavor to the landscape. And no matter where you stood on the island, save for the center, you could see at least one river, and to the tree covered islands beyond.

In the water, I could see boats of all kinds: small boats fitting two paddlers coming from just down river, or larger vessels from distant lands with a full crew and a large store of goods. The port and shoreline was utter chaos; the larger vessels dominated the docks for they had the most goods to load

LEGEND OF FENRIR

and unload, forcing the smaller boats to moor down the coast and walk into the city. And once the vessels were moored and the traders entered the city, the true chaos began. Birca was as busy as the markets in Asgard's capital, Innangard. Traders go to Birca from all sorts of different lands, mostly from places that go by the name of Rome, Constantinople, England, Ireland, Alba, and Francia.

After I disembarked the ship from which I bought passage from Turgu, I made my way into the city, finding the first Norseman I could. When I could finally get to him through the crowd of people and grab his attention, I asked him about the sea serpent. He dismissed me with a wave of his hand. As did the next several men. No one would entertain thoughts of a monster, especially in Birca for that is a place of business and of barter, where negotiations are won by confidence, positioning, and pride. No one had time for stories of a sea serpent and if they entertained the thought, it would weaken their haggling position. But I would not stop.

After receiving a lot of shouting from a burly man with a long beard and a shaved head, I heard a shrill voice call out to me. It came from a skinny man well off in his years with unkempt hair and rotted teeth. On his table sat many jars full of odd smelling liquids and oils. I did not dare ask.

"You search for the sea serpent?" he asked.

"Yes, do you know of it?"

"Of course I know of it. But it is not the serpent you must watch out for, but the dragon. Let me tell you the story of Fa—"

"Nay, old man, I care not for your tales or this 'dragon.' Tell me simply where to find the serpent."

"A fool such as you could not possibly find the serpent. Only I with my unbounded wisdom and sheer cunning can find that slippery, slimy beast."

"…Are you cracked?"

PETER CURSON

"Can a fisherman fish without bait? Can a hunter hunt without a bow? Can—"

Already, I had enough of him. I jumped over his table, took hold of his thinning, brittle hair, and dragged him behind a house to where no one could see us. With a grunt, I threw him to the ground with my hand around his neck. I brought my face so close to him he could smell my horrid breath and I stared into his frightened eyes while I shifted just enough for my fur to rise from my skin and fangs to show, my saliva drooling over his face. "Tell me where."

"South," he stuttered. "South through Gautland all the way to the sea. That is where the serpent swims."

I released him and retracted my fangs. But before I left, I took a jug of ale from behind his table and poured it over his mouth and chest. As I made my way from the marketplace back to the boats, I could hear him raving on about the *Varulv*. But nobody paid him any mind; who would heed the words let alone pay any attention to a cracked, drunk fool?

I used most of the silver I had earned as a merchant to buy a boat that I could paddle alone and enough food to sustain me for a few days—I would not risk hunting in my wolf form this close to Birca and the many water passages. The man from whom I bought the boat spoke with me for a short while. I asked him if he had seen two large wolves, and that I had searched the eastern lands for them, having heard tales of their *Vuko-dlak*. He thought I was as cracked as the old man for spending my days searching for monsters. But if he could make some silver off my adventure, as foolish as it was, he would entertain it. He asked me where I planned to travel next. I told him Gautland, in search of the serpent.

"If your foolish mind leads you through Gautland," he said, "take care not to run into any of the Gautar who call that land home. They do not like us Svear, ever since we did not aid them in the war they faced two years ago against King

LEGEND OF FENRIR

Fairhair of Norvay."

In truth, I cared little for the comings and goings of the Svear or the Gautar, or anyone who names himself "Fairhair." They were neither friend nor foe to me, unless they would aid or attack me. If at all possible, I would choose not to see another human face along my travels. However, the humans do prove resourceful since many of them travel. They may prove useful in finding my sons. As I have seen in my travels, word travels faster than my feet. In any regard, I will not put my trust in them. My greatest chance of success is to find Jor and get his help.

Thus, I set forth from Birca at once and paddled along a southern river, which took me back to the sea. From there, I followed the coastline. I do not think I had ever been more relaxed than those days I spent upon the water. The sky remained blue the entire length, with white clouds sailing overhead carried by the kind breeze. I took to the paddles with leisure so as to not tire my arms. Thankfully, the current took care of my travel on its own, allowing me to fully admire the land of the Norsemen.

Ah, the adventure in my heart was never stronger. Something about those lands resonated with my heart. They did not feel like home, but I felt like I belonged—almost. I would never truly belong anywhere with so many humans. Or any humans for that matter. I cannot properly explain, but any land inhabited by the humans feels claimed and tainted. Would Svealand be free of humans I would gladly spend a length of time exploring its forests and many lakes, after finding Sköll and Hati of course. Yet, Jötunheim ever calls me home.

On the third day of my journey from Birca, my food ran out and I was painfully starved. If I was to continue on my journey at sea rowing for days at a time, I needed to replenish my food stores with a large animal to sustain me. I came upon

PETER CURSON

a river that flowed inland through the middle of a thick forest. No other boats sailed the river and I saw no villages nor any other sign of humans. Deeming it safe, I rowed down the river a short way and moored my boat on the southern shore. At long last, and with great delight, I shifted and began my hunt.

It took until I sniffed out my prey to realize that I had not hunted an animal since before I took on the guise of a human merchant. I have truly missed it. Seeking, finding, chasing, and killing an animal is a thrill unlike any other. Paying a silver coin for food is not only mundane but shameful! However, sacrifices must be made with the necessity of my situation, and all sacrifices will be worth it once I reunite with my sons, even if that means never hunting or shifting again.

I quickly found my rhythm once more for my skill in hunting does not wither over time. Wolves are hunters, there is no changing that. But I was unused to the smells of Svealand and the scents and aromas overwhelmed me, throwing me off course more than once. It is hard to stay on an animal's trail when there are new plants and flowers and trees and leaves to smell! Alas, I set my mind to purpose and tracked a deer down river and as it attempted a drink, I broke cover and brought it a swift and sudden death.

When returning with my deer, I found my boat under search by a couple dozen men whose longboat was moored as well. It was a long, curved ship that curled up in the front and back. A wooden dragon head was mounted on the bow and shields lined the side of the ship, making it one fearsome vessel to any who looked upon it. The men were dressed in leather armor and carried swords and spears with them. The Gautar. I had crossed the border into Gautland.

I decided to leave my boat behind. There was nothing in there I needed and I did not wish to initiate a fight against the Gautar; they could be of help further along in my journey. The men I saw were strong, forged in the fires of battle. If a

LEGEND OF FENRIR

time came when I needed human assistance, it would do me well to ally with them. Even though a sea route to the south would have proved quicker, with the possibility of running into Jor along the way, the land is where I thrive best. And besides, traversing those lands on foot sounded far more pleasurable than spending even another day rowing. So I slunk away from the river with the deer in my mouth and ventured south through the forest, sucking the blood from the deer as I went.

The forest started to thin after two days of trekking, but the land was absolutely and utterly covered in trees. As a predator, especially one as large as me, it made hunting a lot more difficult. But as someone who might have to hide if humans approached, it helped. I could wander in my wolf form without fear of someone seeing me from a far distance. I would know of any human before they knew of me. And if by chance a human was close enough to catch glimpse of me, they would stand in my kill range and never make it out of the forest alive. But I did yearn to exit the forest, even if for a moment to gaze upon open land. Alas, my wish was soon granted.

Only two days after I left my boat behind, I emerged from the woods and found myself atop a small hill overlooking a large field. Finally, open land. I do love the tight embrace of the forest but a particular sense of freedom that comes with open space, especially when looking out from a high vantage point. Beyond this field, the trees spread out over the land in all directions and for a moment, it filled me with despair. Sköll and Hati could be somewhere in the vast array of trees and I could easily pass them. I sighed loudly knowing there was nothing I could do about it. I have a direction and must stick to it.

I took a step to descend the hill but immediately stopped, tilting my head as something triggered my memory.

PETER CURSON

I could not place it though. I looked over the field once more. Twice more. It was… familiar. I knew this place; I had seen it before.
    My heart dropped.
    I sped down the hill onto the field still in my wolf form for at that moment, I did not care who saw me. In only four bounds, I made it to flat ground. I spun around wildly and once I found my bearing, I sprinted. Hard. Until I came to a specific cluster of boulders. Nose in the grass and dirt, I sniffed, my snout leading the rest of my body by pure instinct. This way. No, too far. That way. Yes, I caught the faintest whiff of a scent. The scent drew me to a rather large boulder. There, I saw something.
    I shifted to my normal self and my legs buckled beneath me. Upon my knees, I reached forward. In the ground, half buried and trampled, was a white feather. With my most delicate touch, I removed it from the ground and held it in both hands. I brought it to my nose and smelled it, at once remembering its scent.
    This was the place. This was the place where Kára was struck from the sky by Thor's hand. This was where Kára—the most wonderful of Valkyries—was seen by human eyes and lost her beautiful wings, turning from a Valkyrie to a human herself.
    The scene unfolded before my eyes in an instant. The vicious battle. The Valkyries diving towards the earth, taking the spirits of dead warriors back with them to Valhalla. The storm clouds threatened overhead, peels of thunder ravaging the sky. And I saw him: Thor, the god of Thunder and Lightning. He held his hammer high and summoned forth from the clouds a mighty bolt of lightning. It struck Kára and she crashed to the ground, right at the feet of a human not yet dead. The human laid his hand on hers, staring into her eyes

LEGEND OF FENRIR

with bloodied and wearied eyes. She lost her wings in an instant. In utter confusion and fright, she ran from the battle as fast as her legs could take her with face full of anguish. It is something I can never forget. And it was all my fault.

I tore my eyes from her feather and pounded a boulder with all my might. And I pounded it again. Again. Again. Again. I smelled the blood first for I could not see through my tear-filled eyes. Even as I felt blood pour down my fist and arm I could not stop myself. I screamed loud in great pain for what my life had become. All the misfortune she faced was because of me. A fell and swift doom descends upon any who dare become close to me. Kára was no exception.

Jor. Hél. Kára. Balder. Sköll. Hati.
I am sorry.
I am so sorry.

Legend of Fenrir

Part 2

FOUR

Now I sit here, upon this rock covered in my own blood holding Kára's white feather. All my memories of Asgard come flooding through my mind from the day my siblings and I were captured by Odin and the rest of the High-Æsir to the day I escaped their grasp. I hear Jor's roar as he was thrown through Bifrost's gate in banishment and I see Hél's face go still when Odin pierced her with his spear. I taste Odin's mead and smell the succulent meats the Valkyries served in Valhalla. I see the arrow that pierced Balder and I feel the ocean breeze at his funeral when he was set in his ship for burial at sea. The memories overtake me and I cannot stop them.

It has been one year since I arrived on Midgard, one year since I have seen my wife or my sons. A part of me wishes I could go back to the days Asgard, for even though I was a prisoner there in Innangard's city walls, my family was together. We laughed. We loved one another. We made what merriment we could. Was it not better than all of this? Was it not better to suffer oppression and submission together with

LEGEND OF FENRIR

my family than to live separated like this? We only had to suffer their subjugation until the day the Jötnar army came with war upon their lips. If we could only have waited, Sköll and Hati would still have their mother and father to watch over and raise them instead of wandering the land of the humans alone, living as wolves hiding among the shadows. I should have exercised more caution with them. I should have never let them in Valhalla or anywhere near Thor's pig asses he calls sons. A fool I am. And I let those who I held closest to me down.

Hyrrokkin, my wife, I hope you made it back to Jötunheim without worry. It pains me knowing that after I fled, the Æsir may have set out after you. But you are strong and can take care of yourself. I hope you carry on in my stead. What gives me comfort is that you surely know in your heart that I will do all I can to find our sons. One day we will all be together again. I will find Sköll and Hati and discover how to transcend the cosmos to bring us to you in Jötunheim, my homeland that I have yet to see. I will bring our sons back to you and we will live as one, and fight those who brought this upon us. This I swear.

For the past years, the Jötnar have prepared for war—to attack Asgard and destroy the Æsir once and for all. Hyrrokkin returned to Jötunheim upon my escape in order to aid in the war preparations while my father Loki, though I despise the lineage, remains in Asgard at Odin's table collecting information and sending it back home. It is my hope that I can return in time for the assault. I would leap over the very walls of Innangard, ripping and tearing as I go to the very gates of Valhalla. None would stand against me and survive, even Thor, greatest of the sons of Odin, the Slayer of the Jötnar, would fall before me. I hope he stands against me for I will make a quick death of him. But not Odin. His death will be slow. Painful. And for every agonizing second, he will wish he never punished me. He will wish that he never broke up my family. And he will wish that he left us alone to live our lives. All that has befallen me is because of him and he must face judgement. My judgement.

When the last rays of sunlight fall away from the feather, I lift myself from the rock and kneel in the grass. With my bloodied hands I dig a small hole, placing Kára's feather in after. With my gentlest touch, I replace the dirt and grass overtop. I stop for a moment with my hands holding down the grass and remember her as when I first met her: a radiant creature, beautiful as nature itself, with a kind heart. She saw me as who I was, not as a monster. I was Fenrir, a shapeshifting Jötunn, and that was alright by her. That is how I will remember you, Kára. And hopefully that pleasant memory will overpower the dark thoughts of guilt that haunt me.

Alas it is time to continue. After one last glance backwards, I make my way south into the forest towards my brother. I travel on my two feet this night. I have not spent this many days in my normal form since my days in Asgard. There is a unique simplicity to it. My senses do not flare at the subtlest of things. I do not hear the slight rustling of leaves nor the pattering of small animals. I do not have to smell plants the humans believe to be without scent and I do not have to smell my prey all around me reminding me of my unsatisfied stomach. I can simply walk, look around, and enjoy the stillness of night. Besides, I am far south into Gautland and do not wish to be discovered. It is a surprise I have not yet been. However, now as night deepens to its darkest hour, grogginess besets me.

I climb a thick tree with many boughs, one of the taller ones around. From the top, I can see far in all directions. There it is. To the south, less than another day's march on two feet, is the sea. I will see you soon, brother. It has been far too long since I have heard your voice and dealt with your brash

LEGEND OF FENRIR

attitude, and too long since we used to jest one another and throw insults back in forth, always resulting in our tempers getting the better of us and our inevitable wrestle. I miss those days. But tomorrow I will see you. I wonder how he will react.

Nestling myself halfway down the tree, I fall into a shallow sleep, the kind where my eyes are closed and my mind is at rest, but the moment someone approaches or my ears hear something, I am awake in an instant. Most humans do not possess this quality. Most Jötnar and Æsir do not either. I guess it is just the animal in me.

The morning starts bleak with dark clouds looming overhead. It will probably rain today. A discouragement it is to a traveler, but I do not mind the rain. It brings the world life. The plants drink the water and grow greener and prouder, revitalizing the forest's scent. Rain gives life to the animals. It settles dust, replenishes wells. It quenches the world's thirst. Besides, in a world without rain, no one would appreciate the sun.

The forest soon comes to an end and before me lie fields of tall grass and rocky terrain stretching to the sea now so close. The water: what a sight. There is something about the view of water stretching to the far horizon that comforts me... the unknown quality of it. There could be land right over the edge of the horizon or the sea could simply go on and on to a world unknown. Many courageous Norsemen have set off over the western ocean to explore and discover lands long since dreamed of on the other side. I wonder if they have found anything.

Alas, the quickly growing waves coming into shore bring my thoughts back with them. Nothing disrupts the sea or the landscape around me except for one dwelling made of logs. With a moderate wind blowing across the fields, I approach the home and notice no candles or torches lit inside.

PETER CURSON

However, beside the house on the rocky shore I notice two wooden posts. To one, a wide fishing boat remains tied. The other is vacant.

I approach the window and peer inside. Someone clearly lives here; even in my human form I can smell the man's scent. He lives alone by the smell and look of the place. The fireplace contains a fire nearly reduced to embers. Could the man have gone out on the water with such worrying conditions? A smart man would not.

The wind suddenly howls and thrashes me, and a moment next lightning pierces the sky. Unrelenting peels of thunder ravage my ears and rain falls hard upon my head as though the raindrops had turned to hail. The gale, frigid like those I faced this past winter, sends a chill to my core and I instinctively wish to shift, but I hold back for I am in the open and a human remains unaccounted for. Another roar of thunder erupts from the clouds, unleashing no less than a dozen bolts of lightning upon Midgard. Only once have I witnessed such a sudden storm.

Running around the home with my heart racing alongside my wild thoughts, I look out upon the water. The waves have grown violent and become more so with each passing second. But with the help of the lightning, I can see there in the middle of the water a boat with two men inside, battered by waves from all sides. The man in front holds the sides of the boat in fright. The man in the stern stands tall with a large fishing pole in one hand and something else in his other. My instincts flare and the next moment, it sparks blue. It is the lightning hammer, Mjölnir. And that is Thor.

I rush to the second boat, untie it from its post, and thrust it into the water. I take hold of the oars and propel myself into the raving sea. The waves throw me around but I press on, paddling as best I can. The angry waves have no rhythm to them, coming at me one moment and fleeing the

LEGEND OF FENRIR

next but I somehow manage to keep progressing, peering over my shoulder to find I am indeed nearing them. For the moment, the current is in my favor. I am close enough that despite the thunder and waves, I can hear Thor and the other man yelling. The man is shouting at Thor to bring him back to shore, and that Thor is a madman. But Thor does not respond. Instead, he shouts insults and taunts directed at the water before him. That brain-absent fool. He is fishing for Jormungand.

The line pulls hard and Thor's legs go through the wooden planks of the boat but he does not let go of the pole or his weapon. A moment later, the boat speeds around in circles, led by the fishing pole, creating a maelstrom. It draws all the surrounding water in. Including me. Caught in the quickening current, I paddle hard, gaining on Thor's boat. The man still shouts at Thor in fear and even from here I can see Thor's annoyance and anger. The Thunder God turns and smites the man with Mjölnir, sending him out of the boat with a flash. I speed along the current and watch the man sink into the water, passing his outstretched hand as I go.

As I am mere seconds away from his boat, Thor drops his hammer, taking hold of the pole with both hands and with all of his might, he tugs on the line. His boat comes to a halt and the water before us rips apart. From the depths rises a green, ugly monstrosity if I ever saw one, a serpent of great size rising far into the air with tough scales ominously reflecting the lightning's flashes. My brother, Jor. His roar is loud and full of hate and from his mouth comes the fishing line and he pulls against it hard, trying to break Thor's grasp on the pole but Thor proves to be stronger, his muscles nearly ripping free from beneath his skin. Thor pulls down one last time and manages to topple the giant serpent. As Jor's long body falls to the water, Thor grabs his hammer, about to strike.

"Thor!" I shout, shifting as I leap from my boat—my

PETER CURSON

open jaws aimed for his head. He turns is gaze to me and the disbelief in his eyes strengthens my resolve. He ducks down at the last second, escaping my jaws, yet I fall upon the boat hard, shattering it completely. As I submerge in the water, I swipe at the line and slice it, freeing Jor from our enemy's grasp, and he, too, plunges into the water. Struggling to stay afloat in the weakening maelstrom, I cannot see him or Thor. But then I hear a low rumbling coming from beneath the sea and the waves break way once more. From the water rises Jormungand, knocking Thor high into the air, opening his mouth for a tasty treat. Thor extends his arm and latches onto Jor's tongue and in a feat I would have deemed impossible, he pulls Jor from the waters, swinging him through the air, and hurls him across the water to the rocky shoreline.

Thor lands back in the water but amongst the waves, I cannot find him and I cannot swim in these currents for much longer. Yet as I swim back to the shore, the thunder and lightning cease and the sea begins to reclaim itself. Is the battle now over? What a coward! It seems Thor will only face us with the rest of the High-Æsir at his side. If this is the decision he has made then he only delays his doom.

After reaching land, I pull myself out of the water panting heavily. Even as the waves subside, I cannot see the God of Thunder. He has indeed fled. How unfortunate. Thus, I run down the coast towards Jor, who reverts to his two-legged self, as do I. He struggles to his feet, soaked in water and slime, and looks me up and down.

"What do you think you are doing here?" he asks.

"After over two years, that is what you say to me? Not 'Hello brother, I am glad you are alright, brother'?"

"I ask you that because while I was cast into Midgard's sea from Asgard and while our sister was slain, you remained behind feasting and drinking and humping alongside the Æsir curs who did this to us."

LEGEND OF FENRIR

"Do you think I had a choice? Do you think I wanted to remain there living amongst them? I wanted to kill them! Odin, Thor, those pig's asses Modi and Magni, all of them. Every day I wanted to rip out their entrails one by one and devour them. But I was not able to."

"Because you are weak!"

"I am weak? Was it not I who just saved you from Thor? From a fishing pole? It seems being among the humans have made you weak, brother."

His fists clench tightly and the veins in his arms bulge. But in a moment, they relax, even if only slightly. "You did save me this day, and I am grateful for it. But you are not the brother I once knew. The Fenrir I used to wrestle with would never have suffered captivity by the Æsir nor sat at the same table as our wretched father. He would have never befriended the gods of Asgard, the people who domesticated him like a pet dog. He would have died fighting instead of giving in."

"You speak as if you were there. Do you forget what I am? Jor, a wolf knows one thing well. Survival. That is what I did. I survived. And instead of living as a prisoner, chained up to eat crumbs and scraps, I feasted. Instead of living in hate-filled isolation, I had companions. Yes, the Fenrir you knew would have never befriended an Ás, but that Fenrir was narrow-minded. I learned in Asgard that not all the Æsir are corrupt like Odin and Thor. But I also learned that despite the friends I made there, the Æsir need to be destroyed and their world brought to ruin. So I became a spy, Jor. I took a Jötunn woman to wed, a warrior of great influence in Jötunheim, and we passed information back to our world. Brother, the Jötnar are preparing for war, and I surmise they are close to march as we speak. I am still your brother."

The rain, which had steadily died down after Thor's flee, now completely stops and Jor wipes the water from his face, thinking on my words. "You still have not answered why you are here. If you were a spy and the Jötnar about to set out to war, why are you here?"

"I have two sons, Jor," I say, smiling. He looks at me for a moment and his demeanor loosens. "Sköll and Hati, wolves just like me. But Odin put them to trial, just as he did you, Hél, and me, and he banished them unjustly to Midgard. So I stormed Bifrost and escaped their grasp so I could find them. That is why I am on Midgard, and that is why I am here with you now, brother. I have traveled Midgard for the past year and more but I have not found a trace of them. I have come to see if you knew where they are."

"Fen, I am sorry. I do not know where they are."

"Have you heard any rumors of them? Two large wolves?"

He shakes his head. "Just what some travelers name the *Varulv*, which I now presume is you. They speak about you quite a bit. And it seems your tales have reached even the gods of Asgard. Thor was shouting for me to tell him where you were. They are looking for you."

"Let them look."

"Stouthearted you are, but caution this news. If they want to find you, they may also look for your sons in order to draw you out. Find your boys, Fenrir. Find them quickly."

"Will you not help me?"

He looks at me hard for a while and turns, walking back to the water. "I will not be going anywhere with you. The sea is the only home I have left, and I will not leave it. But as thanks for saving me this day, I will tell you this: if anyone or anything on Midgard knows where your sons are, it will be Huginn and Muninn."

Of course, Odin's ravens who scour the earth for information about the humans. How did I not think of them sooner?

"And Fenrir, I will keep an ear out for word of my

LEGEND OF FENRIR

brother-sons." I nod and he turns his back to me, diving into the water, shifting as he goes. The water ripples as he enters and a second later, I see the last of his green tail slithers into the deep. Though I still do not know where my sons are or whether they are even safe, I have direction in my search. Now, how do I find Huginn and Muninn?

FIVE

Much planning must go into catching those two peeving ravens. First, I have to think up a way to find them. Second, I must conceive a trap to ensnare them. And third, I will need to make them tell me all the know. Three problems lie before me and I must solve them quickly, but how can I even begin to solve the first? If I cannot find two giant wolves on this earth, how will I be able to find two ravens? And though I would search endlessly across this earth for the ravens and my sons, I fear I never would find them. Yet for all my misfortune, there remains one patch of blue in this sky of cloud, one glimmer of hope in a starless night: Thor knows I am here in the North. Under any other circumstance, this would prove a hinderance. However, with my whereabouts known to the *veslingr*, he will relay this information back to Odin, who will in turn dispatch his ravens to scour these lands until they find me. And now as I swim in one of Gautland's many lakes to rid myself of the smell and slime of sea water, I discover the solution to my first

LEGEND OF FENRIR

problem. I will not find Huginn and Muninn, I will allow them to find me.

If I am to take this route, I will have to ready my plan and set it into motion with all haste, for it will not just be those ravens searching for me. Thor will be hunting me as well, most likely with his sons Modi and Magni. And perhaps his half-brothers Vidar and Vali. Those five Æsir hated me more than the rest of their people combined. It would not be a fight I could win. Thor is the strongest of all the Æsir, with his half-brothers not far behind. And despite their young age, Modi and Magni have all the makings to become even stronger than their father. Need I any more reasons to put my plan into motion as soon as possible? I wade to shore and make my way westward.

I spend the next four days traveling west looking for the perfect location to set my trap. If a location looks promising, I investigate it from top to bottom and from all angles, including from the branches of the trees, for where else will ravens perch themselves? If a location gives me even the slightest worry, I move on for if there is any gap that the ravens could exploit, they will. There is no room for mistakes. This plan cannot fail. But as I trudge on, no location proves suitable. Time presses at my back as if it was one of the gods itself and I feel my paranoia taking hold of my mind. Even still, I will not settle for a location if it has the slightest chance of failure. I must keep moving. Finally, on the evening of the fourth day, after scouring and abandoning five unsuitable locations, I find a place that will work.

Before me rises a small hill in the middle of this sea of trees in which a bear has made its den. It soon becomes my den. With my stomach full, I go to work digging out this hole large enough for me to comfortably rest inside, which is no easy task. But with the pressing fear knowing I am now being

PETER CURSON

hunted, I finish the task quicker than expected. When complete, I rake in lots of leaves to form my bed. This night I spend under the hill, protected from wind and unfriendly eyes. After five minutes trying to sleep with irritating insects and bugs crawling all over me, I shift into my normal self. I cannot stand bugs in my fur, crawling, gnawing, nestling themselves deep in my coat. At times, they anger me more than the Æsir. At least in my normal form, I can slap them away, and they have no place to make home. Although, my bare skin is not used to the exposure of the night and I sleep with a chill, even if a warm summer night it is. My thoughts go back to the days I spent in Innangard. Since I was forbidden to shift into my wolf form, I slept my nights in a bed with warm blankets and furs. It was nice, with a unique feeling of comfort I just cannot reach as a wolf. There is something about being wrapped in a tight, warm embrace that makes my slumbers all the more restful.

 In the morning, I leave my den and make my way ever westward, my sons upon my mind with each step. I have forgotten that they very well could be in this forest, hiding away. My quest to find Jor and now to catch the ravens have distracted me from looking for their tracks or sniffing for their scents. How terrible it would be if I had passed them by during yesterday's march. If only they knew I was here in this world searching for them. Oh, what I would give for them to just know this. What if they think I forsook them like Loki forsook my siblings and I on that dreaded day? Sköll and Hati do not know I defied Odin to get here. They do not know I have ceaselessly wandered Midgard's treacherous North to find them. My sons, do not give up on me for I have not given up on you. I will not give up on you.

 At just past midday, I exit the forest and see close by a large fortress city on the shore of a narrow strait. Many boats

LEGEND OF FENRIR

moor there with many more traveling to and from the land across the water. Some even travel north or south set upon longer voyages. This is the perfect place to begin. I shift to my normal self and head straight for the city.

A troop of warriors guarding the eastern gate stop me and ask me from where I hail. It is time to initiate my plan.

"I live three days east of here," I say, "on the shore of the sea."

"A long way you have come without pack, food, or supplies," the leader of the troop says. "What is the purpose of your travel to Hälsingborg?"

"Great misfortune, one which you would not believe if I told you."

"Unless you do tell me, I will not allow you through these gates."

I deliberately hesitate with my response, looking each man in the eye, showing my apparent fright. "Very well. I was chased from my home and pursued as I fled west through the forests. It followed me for two days until I finally lost it."

"It?"

"A giant wolf, black as night, five times the size of any bear. I had heard rumors of the beast but did not believe them to be true until I saw it with my own eyes and smelled its horrid breath. They call it the *Varulv*."

The leader looks at me with a hardened face, clearly not believing in my story. But I notice one of his men feeling uneasy. I turn to him and ask if he has seen it.

"No, I have not seen it, but many of the travelers speak of it, along with the sea serpent."

"A great mercy it is that you have not encountered it—or that it encountered you. A greater mercy that I escaped. That is why I am here, so I can collect food and supplies and flee these lands, if you will allow me through."

The leader looks at me for another few moments but

PETER CURSON

his resolve shifts. "Are we in danger here? Is the city safe?" I take a look around. "This city has high walls and it seems to hold many warriors inside. I do not think the Wolf would attack, but who knows what that crazed beast will do? You should prepare for an attack nonetheless. And by no circumstances should you allow anyone to travel into the eastern forests lest they become food for the beast."

The warriors allow me through and they close the gate behind me. Before I can thank him, the leader sets off to the heart of the city, presumably to tell the city's jarl all that he has learned. This is going perfectly.

Without a second thought, I make my way to the marketplace and begin conversing with the people and merchants there, just as I used to before I set out for Svealand and now here in Gautland. I even stole some trinkets from an elderly man when he was not looking so I could barter with more people. I have almost forgotten how strong a haggler I am, for with those few trinkets, I traded and continued to trade until I held in my possession an arm ring and a bottle of wine, though, it was not a great bottle of wine.

All the while, I spread word of the *Varulv*, who claimed the eastern forest as his territory. I was not sure what to expect since those who I met in Birca, even as traveling merchants, were courageous and hardened people. Perhaps the news would not phase them, especially if their paths lead only by way of water. Yet even only hours after entering the city, the town's watch had more than doubled, filling the town with anxiety and unease.

After I spread the news around Hälsingborg's marketplaces, I left the city southward before they too closed that gate and traveled upon a main road, warning any travelers of the Wolf as I went. Soon, I came to a city named Lund, repeating my activities there and then through an old town by the name of Uppåkra, all the way to a southern town called

LEGEND OF FENRIR

Trelleborg. Yet at each town, the *Varulv* followed me. It was no longer just outside Hälsingborg but outside of their own cities—a threat of immediate danger. Each city prepared for an attack by the Wolf and the townspeople were frightened. Some of them even departed the cities in fear. What better way to spread the news of my whereabouts? I am sure that even the lands far south of here will hear of the treacherous *Varulv* soon enough.

After my success in Trelleborg, I make haste northward back to my den for Huginn and Muninn will soon hear these rumors pass over human's lips in fearful whispers and they will search the forest until they find me. And find me they will.

Upon returning to my den, I begin preparations immediately; I cannot afford to let any time slip by unused. I shift to my normal self and reach into the large sack I took from a fishing boat in Hälsingborg and pull out a large fishing net. Climbing the hill to the top of my den's entrance, I secure the net and then conceal it with plants and leaves. Last, I attach a rope, also concealing it as it dangles down to the entrance of the den. Simple, primitive, but it will do.

Before retiring, I shift and scour the forest. If I am to await the coming of two crows that could be as close as Svealand or as far as the southern regions of Midgard, I will need food. It takes me a couple of hours but I find a bear and hunt it with relative ease. A strong urge it is to devour it here and now, but I must be smart and savor my game for as long as I can. So I return to my den after a successful hunt and collapse onto my bedding. Alas, it is time to wait.

Since I conceived this plan, I have looked forward to this time where I would have nothing to do but wait for the two birds. But here only on the second day of waiting, it has become evident I have lost all virtue of patience. The days where I could sit in the forest alone for hours on end with nothing but the smells and sounds and my own thoughts to occupy myself have long since passed me by. In the place of patience, all that is left is anxiousness; only one thing rests in my mind, all-consuming, and it does not come nearly as fast as I would hope. And the thought that I might have found my sons if I had continued my search instead of deviating to catch Odin's ravens picks away at my resolve shred by painful shred.

What would Hél tell me if she was here? Well, now as the Demoness of the Dead, Ruler of Hélheim, I do not know what she would say. But as my sister whom I once knew and cherished, the cleverest of us three siblings, she might tell me that a cunning plan has a better chance at success than aimless wandering, and that a fortnight to construct such a plan, as long as it may seem, is shorter still than a month or year or decade of directionless roaming. That is, if my plan is successful. I will need to make them tell me all they know, if they know anything at all. Thus, doubt enters my mind again for if Huginn and Muninn knew where my sons were, the gods could have captured them by now and used them as bait just like Jor had said. Oh, what I would do to rid myself of these agonizing thoughts and be able to simply enjoy the stillness of nature. What I would do to have my sons beside me.

My ear twitches. Something in the near distance. A familiar noise and yet distinct. Two caws, one answering the other. But they were not the caws of some common crow or raven. Nay. Huginn and Muninn are here.

I shift to my normal self and run out of my den. I rush to the side and conceal myself within some bushes at the foot of the knoll and before I can blink thrice, two ravens, double the size of those here on Midgard, swoop down from the canopy and perch themselves on a branch overlooking my den. They look at the entrance, scan the area, then look at the entrance again. What are they waiting for? Surely they must suspect a trap; they have seen too much here in the world of the

LEGEND OF FENRIR

humans to be so naïve. In any regard, they cannot simply move on in their search without knowing for certain if I am in there or not. And so they dive down and into the den. I dash to the rope and heave. The bottom of the net falls over the entrance of the den and moments later, Huginn and Muninn fly into it, causing the rest of the net to fall after it. Their shrieks fill the air, piercing my ears like sharp knives. They are caught! I shift and pounce atop the net so that they cannot free themselves and clamp my jaws around them, just enough for them to feel the sharpness of my teeth. I wrap the net around them this way and that, their wings and feathers caught and distorted ten times over, and when I am satisfied, I toss them into my den and walk in, allowing malice to take over.

"Fenrir, you must not harm us!" cawed Huginn.

"Yes, must not harm us!" echoed Muginn.

"That is a decision for you to make," I reply. "And the decision lies before you now. Tell me where my sons are. Tell me what you know of Sköll and Hati and I will release you. Fail to tell me what you know and I will pluck you feather by foul feather, cook you over a roaring fire, rip your flesh from your bones and pick my teeth with your beaks."

The ravens struggle in the net attempting to cut themselves free with their talons and beaks but to no avail. Three moments pass without their confessions, and my patience reaches its end. I pounce upon them, smashing them with my paw and hold them there. "Where are my sons!"

"We will not say!"

"No, we will not!"

"Without us, you will never find them."

"You will never find them if you kill us."

I know they are correct. And they know I know. They think they have the advantage despite their capture, but it is not so. "You are correct: I cannot kill you both... but I can kill one of you. Which one of you will it be?" I dig my claws

into their necks and they squawk with fright. "Will it be you Huginn? Will it be your head I send back to Odin in your brother's mouth?" I move my head to Muninn and run my slick tongue over his body, leaving him drenched in my drool. "Oh, you are tasty. Perhaps it will be you, Muninn. Your time is up. It ends now."
"Stop! We will tell!"
"Yes, we will tell!"
I take myself from them, allowing them to breathe and reclaim themselves.
"Sköll and Hati are in Svealand."
"Yes, in the forest surrounding Hämnd."
"They have begun terrorizing the citizens."
"And Sigurd has been sent to slay them."
I release myself from them and they remain still awaiting my response. Hämnd, as close as Svealand. What joyous news. They terrorize the citizens? Due to the anger set in their hearts by the Æsir no doubt and the power they now hold over the weak humans. Though, I have seen the Einherjar army and they hold many heroes and strong warriors. I must find them.
"Sigurd, who is he?"
"He is the son of the hero Sigmund," Huginn starts.
"And the son of Hjordis, wife of King Alf of Svealand," Muginn finishes.
"Why was he chosen to kill my sons?" I ask.
"We do not know."
"Allfather does not tell us all he knows."
I am not sure if I believe their words, but in this moment, I care not for who Sigurd is and why he was chosen. Son of a hero, a hero himself, I do not care because now I know where my sons are. Hämnd. I must leave at once.
With a swipe of my paw, I rip apart the net, pulling out many of their feathers and they are sure to let me know their pain, and it gladdens my quickening heart. But before I

LEGEND OF FENRIR

allow them to escape, I leave them with a message: "You have been flying these skies for over a year and could not find me. Do not think I will not go back into hiding. And I assure you, you nor the gods of Asgard will ever find us. Your master has destroyed my life and split my family apart. But no longer. I will find my sons and there is nothing Odin can do to stop me." I move aside and the ravens burst into flight out of the cave and their caws of fright and warning are lost in the wind.

ᛋᛁᛪ

SIX My journey northward across Gautland was quick. I moved day and night, forgoing meals to reach Svealand quickly and from there I could find where Hämnd stood. I avoided all interaction with the Gautar so as to not hamper my progress. Although, at times when I found a town, I would stop to visit an inn where I could refill my stomach with prepared and cooked foods. And of course quench my thirst with a hearty ale or mug of mead. And even if I finished my meal late into the evening, I would take my leave of the town and continue my journey, not stopping until the moon was well into the sky to make up the time I lost.

What joy does direction bring! The fog of doubt and despair no longer haunt my steps. My mind does not wander. My feet do not falter. My sons are alive and they are close. Just over a week it has been since I set out to Hämnd. I crossed into Svealand not but three days ago and found my way to the nearest village. They could not help me except by pointing me to the next northward town. This one is larger and stood on the shore of a large lake. It serves as a waypoint between the eastern lands of Svealand and the western nation of Norvay,

LEGEND OF FENRIR

and thus proves to be a bustling market town full of merchants, travelers, and also many thieves and questionable folk. While under the guise of a traveling merchant, as I have become well accustomed, I learned Hämnd was just a two days journey north through the forests upon horseback—one for me. I slipped away from the town with minimal interaction, for even though I can pass as human easily enough, I am larger than them. Only their tallest and biggest men can measure up against me. Even the slightest babble of an unusually large man could reach the ears of Huginn and Muninn and I would not have them find me before I reach Hämnd and reunite with my sons.

    I journeyed into the night not slowing a pace. I would not delay the reunion even a minute if I could help it. I did stop for the briefest moment when a family of deer strode into my view, and even then they fled northward towards Hämnd. A pleasant hunt it was. If it were not for those deer, I would not have eaten for an entire day. I ate my fill and with a satisfied stomach, my mind reclaimed its rationale. I decided to rest for the night under the cloudy sky. Now here I lie in a small glade with my belly full of food and my heart full of anticipation.

    Tomorrow.

    I will reunite with my sons tomorrow. In the morning, I will pay this town a visit. Sköll and Hati have terrorized the citizens so they surely must make their home close by in these surrounding forests just like the ravens said, and I have no doubt the citizens know their exact whereabouts, even if only through hushed rumors. I can see them now: cowering within their town, scared to step outside the safety of their homes. They no longer go out to hunt lest they be hunted. They no longer explore the forest for the forest is no longer theirs.

    Yet, what shall we do once I reunite with my sons? I would much like to keep to the forest which they have now

PETER CURSON

claimed. It has been far too long without my own territory to hold, roam, and protect. But if Huginn and Muninn knows we are here, all of the gods know we are here. We cannot stay. We must leave this place. Perhaps we can journey back the way I came. The remote and desolate mountains east of here, though treacherous, would make as a perfect escape route. There remain many places to hide in those lands with treacherous weather in the winter, which we can easily handle but two pesky ravens could not. Perhaps we could go back to Xwayxway. The mountains and animals there are bountiful and my only friend on Midgard is there.

    I hope with all sincerity that rumor of my exploits in those lands near Xwayxway have not reached the ravens' ears. I would keep them from the affairs of my punishment and of the gods so as to not disturb their way of life. They are a people set in their way of tradition and peace, lest others make enemies of them. They do not deserve the misfortune that follows me closer than my own shadow. Even if the ravens do not know of my time in Xwayxway, it would not take long for them to find out if my sons and I returned to live there. Be it a year or even ten, they would find us. It seems that maybe there is no place for us here. Nay, we must find our way back to Jötunheim somehow, but that is a problem for another day. There is only one thing that matters before me: our reunion.

    But what of Sigurd, the man who sets out to slay my sons? Surely anyone who is chosen to kill Sköll and Hati must be a renowned warrior. And the King has chosen him no less. I will keep my wits about me but will not fret. He is a human. We are Jötunn. We cannot be stopped.

    There will be no sleep this night. Not for me. Although weary, my mind will not allow me to sleep. With head between my paws in the dirt and fallen leaves, I rest my eyes but remain alert and spend the remaining hours of the night thinking of Sköll and Hati. I hope they have grown big and

LEGEND OF FENRIR

strong. And I hope they will receive me with open arms. I have lost my ties with Jor; he has gone his own way. I do not know what I would do if Sköll and Hati reject me and go their own way. But that thought is quick to leave my mind. That will not happen. They are my sons. We will be together again. Tomorrow.

  A blanket of fog had rolled in during the night leaving the day dark and gloomy. But it made my approach to Hämnd quick and easy. Never have I seen a town such as this. At first, I thought it abandoned for I could not see any people nor hear anything but the wind. Yet, I could smell them. Putrid. It seems they do not bathe for they would have to venture out into the forest to do so. They are here, and they are scared. Splendid.

  In my normal form, I walk into town and immediately my instincts flare, alerting me to many presences. I am under watch. Alone, I look around and see the townsfolk peering at me from their homes, eyes wide with fright. The market and well are deserted and still I see no one. As I continue, the wind brings to my ears a sound repeating over and over. The sound of chopping wood. I carry on towards the sound with more and more eyes watching as I go. When I reach the home, there stands a man with back turned to me swinging a mighty axe. I wait until he swings down and call out to him. He dislodges his axe and faces me with all intent to attack.

  "Who are you?" he asks from behind his frizzled beard.

  "A traveler looking for food," I reply. "Though, the market stands empty. Why do the people remain indoors when the day remains dry?"

  He looked behind me and then all around. "How did you get here?"

  "Not that it is any of your concern, I walked north

PETER CURSON

through the forest."

"Nay, it is not my concern, but safety should be yours. You have doomed yourself, traveler. The *Varulvs* stalk these forests. Our town has suffered many attacks from them. They do not plunder. They do not take our food. They come to kill. The first day they raided and destroyed our crop and homes. The second they took twenty lives. Yet on the third, they did not take any. They did not show themselves. Thinking they had moved on or rested that night, the townsfolk decided to escape. They walked straight into their jaws. They are cunning, these beasts."

"A griping tale. However, I made it here unharmed. I will not be so quick to believe such tales of monsters and beasts."

"If you do not believe me, believe King Alf. Yesterday, Sigurd, son of Sigmund, and his men rode into town on the King's order to rid us of those monsters."

"Sigurd is here?"

"Nay, I saw him off not but an hour ago."

"Which way did he go?"

"You do not think of following him into the forest? That would be madness. You should stay here and wait until Sigurd brings back the heads of those wolves."

I do not hear his last words for my eyes fixate on the ground. Many horses have ridden here. If it were not for my small nose, I would have picked up their scent already. But now I must give chase. Without another look, I take off following the horse tracks out of the town and into the misty forest. It is easy to follow them for here the trees are congested with undergrowth covering the ground. The horses trampled their own trail through the forest. Not yet shifted, I carry on through the forest further north, and then east until I come to a wide path strewn with the corpses of a dozen men and their horses. With the warriors dismembered and disemboweled,

LEGEND OF FENRIR

the path lies cluttered with limbs and innards, and pools of blood spot the ground. The man closest to me—what is left of him—only his upper half remains. Where his legs are, I cannot see. Large chunks are missing from the horses' hides and some are even headless. Only two things on Midgard could have done this. Well, three, but it was not by my jaws that they met their fate. Tracks lead further east along the path, large tracks made by the paws of my sons. But a single set of horse tracks travel in the same direction with all haste. But something is wrong. The horse does not seem to be fleeing the wolves. It chases them.

    I shift at once and in an instant, I smell them. My sons. Filtering out the blood and guts and horse shit, I breathe deep and focus on them. Though my eyes can see these are their tracks, my nose confirms it in my heart, and I take off down the path, no longer following Sköll and Hati by sight, but by smell. My instincts flare so strongly I can barely keep hold of my mind. I focus on the smell of my sons and the sounds of the forest. It is silent, which worries me. Would I but hear the sound of battle, of a man shouting, his horse whining, or my sons barking. An urge in me beckons to howl, to let my sons know I am here and that I am coming, but I will not warn Sigurd of another predator and sginal his escape. Odin, prepare your tables for another guest. Sigurd dies today.

    I come to a bend in the path and as I round it, I hear a distinct sound that causes my heart to sink: a piercing whimper. Hati. I push harder and three strides next, I see them. Away from his horse, a human stands tall in battle dress with a sword with steel glowing red. He stands against two large beasts, wolves, almost as large as me. But the sight is not joyous. Hati lies on the ground bleeding from a grievous wound, alive yet badly hurt, and Sköll stands protecting him, panting and with many lacerations marring his body. Sköll sees me at once as I charge for Sigurd and unleash a roar that shakes him to his core. He spins on his heels and sees death rushing towards him. I pounce and snap my jaw but he is quick to lunge out of the way, landing hard on the ground. Digging in my paws, I turn and pounce again. He rolls. I swipe. He ducks. And I lunge, yet he does not dodge. Sigurd stands his ground and swings his sword with unimaginable speed and slices my chest with such force it sends me flying backwards through the air. Before I know it, I land at Sköll's feet and struggle to regain my stance. Unimaginable pain afflicts my chest. What in the Nine Worlds was that? It felt as though I had been struck with the force of a hundred bears. What kind of sword does this human wield to send me in my enormous size flying through the air?

"Father?" Sköll says with such disbelief it rips my heart asunder.

I do not reply; I will not divert my attention from a foe with a magicked weapon. Sigurd stands tall and strong, larger than most humans I have seen. His garb is fair, kingly and yet ready for battle. He does not wear leather armor like his men, but fine iron mail, which by how he fights seems to weigh him down little. Over his shoulders is draped the pelt of an adolescent bear and behind him flows a regal cape lined with golden patterns. Foster-son of the King indeed. Son of a hero. Yet a hero himself, that remains to be seen.

His eyes, despite the fearlessness and fortitude they hold, show confusion. First, there was only one *Varulv* in the east, then two here in Svealand, and now three. Further yet, I detect fright—I can smell it in his sweat. His jaw clenches behind a trimmed beard, and his hair, braided, reaches far down his back. He stands at the ready, sword directed straight at me. The sword bears an ethereal red glow, radiating and pulsing with each of Sigurd's breaths. The sword has been welded with intricate patterns in its iron, the like of which many of the Einherjar wield. Yet neither the glow nor the patterns are what

LEGEND OF FENRIR

draw my attention. What draws my eyes are distinct markings along the blade:

ᚱᚦᚾᚲᚾ

The markings themselves seem to be the source of the red aura. But a magical blade will not deter me. My foe stands before me and he will fall.

"Who are you?" Sigurd asks.

"Pain, death, and chaos. I am the one who will deliver you from this world. I am the *Varulv*."

"Do you carry a name, beast? One that the humans did not give you?"

"My name matters not, Sigurd of the Norsemen. All that should concern you is my appetite."

"Very well, *Varulv*. By your move."

Sköll steps up next to me growling from deep within himself. His fur brushes against mine unleashing a powerful instinct from deep within me: protection. I burst forward with all my might, a wave of pain coursing from my cut, and Sköll follows instantly. We charge down the path at our foe head-on. At the last second, we break off left and right and jump back against Sigurd. He rolls forward and recovers to his feet and moves against Sköll. My son dances left and right, faking attack, luring Sigurd in. Sigurd lunges and as he does, I run in. He is aware of me and swings his sword. I evade then pounce, but cannot land a strike. Sköll maneuvers around me and we beset him with many attacks yet he proves to be one elusive foe. I check back on Hati. He arches his head to see us fight. His eyes meet mine and, despite his agonizing wound, I can see joy in them. He fills me with strength. With his brother, I continue our relentless assault and do not give this human one opportunity to attack. A stalemate this is, which is favorable because I will outlast him. He will overstep. Overreach. He will falter and when he does, I will rip him apart.

Sigurd dodges a swipe from Sköll's paw and manages to gain some distance from the two of us, but as he does, his foot catches a root in the ground and he stumbles. My legs instinctively go to pounce but I catch a gleam in Sigurd's eye and stop myself. But Sköll pounces. Sigurd's grip tightens. I shout after my son and I leap for him to hold him back but he escapes my reach. I see a flash of red and Sköll hurdles through the air. The ground shakes from his fall. He rolls in the dirt colliding with Hati and does not get up. I look back to Sigurd and see him hunched over, holding his sword arm. I smell his blood. Sköll struck him hard. His sword hangs loosely in his hand and in his eyes I can see the realization of defeat. He cannot contest me with an injured arm. He steps away from me and towards his horse with all appearances of fleeing.

"They are badly hurt," he says.

"As are you."

"Indeed, I cannot continue this fight. However, your sons' wounds are grievous indeed," he says looking up between the trees, seeing the afternoon sky. "I surmise they will not survive to see nightfall without aid."

I take a glance back and see Sköll panting heavily and Hati trying to raise himself, only to collapse in pain.

"I am leaving, *Varulv*. The choice remains before you: hunt me down or aid your sons. I look forward to your decision." He spins on his heels and sprints to his horse. I dash after him but he reaches his horse and kicks off through the trees where I cannot follow in my wolf form. It will not take him long to reach the town upon horseback and thereafter, he will be lost to me. Yet my choice is simple.

LEGEND OF FENRIR

I rush for Sköll and Hati. Now beside them, I see how terrible their wounds are. A gash runs down Hati's underbelly so wide I can see his intestines, which give off a putrid stink. Blood runs down his fur. So much blood. Sköll's large gash runs down his flank with many more covering the rest of his body from muzzle to paw. I drop down beside them and they crawl over, burrowing their heads into my chest. Sköll knows it is me, but Hati sniffs me to be sure.

"I am here now. I am here."

"Father," Hati says struggling to keep his eyes open to look at me. The pain is too much to bear. "How?"

"I escaped. When Odin banished you, I broke free of their grasps. Your mother and Týr helped me escape across the Rainbow Bridge. I would not forsake you. I would not abandon you. Many hundreds of leagues over this world I have traveled to find you two. I never stopped searching. Never. You have to know I never stopped. You have to know."

Sköll coils from the pain of his wounds, which anchors me back to the situation before me. "Shift, my sons; I will carry you to the town and get you help." When they shift, their pain multiplies and they let out hoarse screams. I shift as well and lift their naked bodies over my shoulders and trudge through the undergrowth towards Hämnd. Each step I take sends a jolt of pain surging through my sons and it pains me to hear their suffering but I cannot help them here. Tree roots attempt to trip me and the many bushes grasp at my ankles and with each step my sons become heavier and heavier. But I will carry on and toil through the forest as the sweat on my brow meet the tears upon my cheeks.

We emerge from the tree line near sundown. I see no one outside of their homes, which is expected if they have learned that even Sigurd, son of Sigmund, has fled from not just two great wolves, but three. With knees weak and wounds

PETER CURSON

stinging, I approach the town without thought of anything thereafter. I just need to reach the town and they will be fine. As soon I am in ear shot, I shout for a healer. No one answers. Now between the first homes, I shout louder. "Help! I need a healer. Somebody help me!" The man I spoke with earlier in the day cautiously looks out from his home with his axe in hand and upon seeing me with my sons hanging off my shoulders, he repeats my call for the healer. An aging woman with two others younger than her make their way to us with rags and many herbs. Behind them, the rest of the townsfolk slowly trickle into the street but once I meet the healers, all else fades from the world and my eyes fixate on Sköll and Hati's faces riddled with pain.

"What did this?" the man asks.

"The *Varuhs*," I reply.

"Sigurd fled from the wolves," he says as the women work at cleaning the blood and dirt from their wounds and applying their herbs before attempting to close my sons' wounds. "Before Sigurd took leave of this town, he warned us that three wolves stalk our forest."

"Yes, I was with Sigurd when he found them. We were the only ones to escape." The women continue to tend my sons' wounds with trembling hands, yet in the elderly woman's face I see both worry and confusion. She looks to the man. "I have never dealt with wounds this severe before. There is nothing I can do."

"You must do all you can!" I shout, causing her to shake. She stands and approaches the man to whisper something in his ear. Yet my hearing surpasses their own even in this form, so I hear her hushed words. "These wounds are not like the others attacked by the wolves. They were caused by the stroke of a sword."

The man puts the story together almost instantly. Even if he does not yet know of our ability, he knows that

LEGEND OF FENRIR

Sigurd dealt these wounds—and an enemy of Sigurd is an enemy of theirs.

"Kill them!" he shouts swinging his axe. I grab it by the handle, ripping it from his hands, and strike him down. Before anyone else can react, I plant myself in the ground and shift, unleashing a howl never before heard in this world. The townsfolk scream in utter terror and flee in all directions from me. I look down at my sons and no longer know what to do. I do not know what to do. Nay, they cannot stay here so I must get them help from the town I passed two days back. I fall to the ground and roll on my side. Sköll and Hati grasp my fur hard and I roll myself up, throwing them over my back. In seconds, I race down the path and into the forest heading south.

Darkness looms over the forest as the sun nears the horizon. Making my way between the trees proves difficult for I am too large to maneuver around them, especially with my sons upon my back. Not a single thought crosses my mind. I keep them back. All there is is the forest before me and the need to find help. I will find the town and they will know what to do. They will save my sons.

"Father," Hati moans as I feel his grip loosening. "I… I cannot hold on." He slips off my back and lands in the grass.

I drop down beside him and call his name. "Get back on! It is not much further." But Sköll releases his grip and falls next to his brother. "Sköll. No. Hold onto me. Just hold on. You will be alright; I will save you both."

Sköll's eyes shut tight but when he opens them and looks at me, I see in them something I have not seen before. His resolve has diminished. His strength faded. And now… there remains nothing but resignation. Hati lies on his back holding a rag to his wound but soon releases it, foregoing all attempt at survival. My knees buckle and I fall in between

PETER CURSON

them, their heads beside mine.

"It is so cold," Sköll says, shivering.

My voice catches in my throat for I know that this is it. "Shift, my sons. Be strong. Be strong for me." Sköll and Hati hear my words and they shift, their muzzles touching my own as they lay on their sides. Their panting is slow and weak. Their nostrils no longer flare. Their tails go limp.

"Look Hati," Sköll says looking west. "Look at the sun. It is… so warm. I have always loved the sun…"

"I do not know of what you speak," Hati replies. "Up. Look up. The moon… it is so gentle… so… calm."

Their panting ceases.

Their chests rise and fall no more.

They are gone.

SEVEN

Night falls upon Hämnd. The moon hides behind the cover of dark clouds. Mist falls upon the town, contained by the forest. And that is when I appear, a dark figure in the fog. Swift as a shadow I advance. I begin with their homes. With merciless hate I destroy them, tearing them down to their foundations and the screams of fear fill the night. The people run in all directions but they will not escape me. The first humans I encounter, I gnaw in half, throwing their carcasses in the street for all to see. Not all of them flee yet——some grab axes and spades, but I cannot be stopped. I rip the people limb from limb and send their heads rolling down the street. Their shrieks consume me. Their blood floods from my mouth and flesh from my teeth. They come at me from all sides casting chains over me and around my neck yet the humans are weak. I yank the chains from their grasps and kill them in every way I can. I trample them. Claw them. Eat them. Decapitate them. Drag them into the ground. Throw them in the fires. I do not stop. Every man, woman, and child must die. The young, the

PETER CURSON

elderly, the sick. They try to fight; I kill them. They try to hide; I find them. They try to flee; I hunt them. They curse me and I laugh. They beg for mercy and I laugh louder. It is pitiful how weak they are. Slow, witless beings every last one of them. Their tears bring me joy and their pain furthers my ferocity. Where is Sigurd now? Where are the King's men? Where are the gods of Asgard? None will stop me. None can stop me. My hunger is not satisfied. My thirst not quenched. And so I continue my onslaught, ripping and tearing, gnawing and hacking until I am drenched in their blood and covered in their guts. And slowly, as the night wanes and dawn approaches, their screams are lost to the world, not one of them yet among the living, and I return to the forest seething for more.

With human blood drying upon my fur, I appear back at the glade where my sons lie. I cannot bear to look at them. Not yet. I simply cannot face it. As if guided by another being, I immediately begin to dig. The soil is cold and riddled with worms but I neither grimace at the cold nor flinch when I scrape my claws against the boulders in the ground. There is nothing except the grave I dig. And with each swipe of my paw, I shed another tear. I pick up my speed. Whereas I started this task slow and dreadful, I now dig as fast as my legs will allow. I dig deep until I can fit inside, and then wider until I can fit twice over.

This was the easy part.

My paws are raw and my legs ache. I can barely lift myself out of the hole. I walk to the middle of the glade but keep my head turned. I know I will have to bring myself to look at them but it is too much to bear. Yet I cannot drag this out any longer. I close my eyes and feel for my sons. I bump my muzzle against Sköll and feel for his mane. I bite down and drag him to the hole and with a moan, I cast him in. I sniff out Hati and pull him over. I open my eyes to let the tears fall and

LEGEND OF FENRIR

look at everything but my son. The trees, the leaves, the roots on the ground. But I catch a glimpse of Hati's hindlegs dragging in the dirt void of life and my legs give in. I push back but I fall again. Yet I push and push until I reach the hole and with a wail, I cast my second son into his grave.

I stand here, not allowing my eyes to fall, still resisting. What father could withstand the sight of their fallen children? But I cannot simply turn my back without seeing their faces one last time. I know in my heart I must do this. So I bring my eyes down and see them there. Lifeless. Motionless. My chest heaves and my stomach churns.

"Sköll, Hati, I failed you. I will never forgive myself for what has happened to you. If only I was quicker. If only I was stronger. I could have protected you. I could have saved you. I am sorry..." Anguish consumes me, staying my voice, and all I can do to alleviate the pain is let loose a loud, pain-ridden howl.

Sleep eludes me.

It did not take me long to bury my sons. I thought the sooner I finished it, the sooner the pain would stop. I was wrong. I cannot bring myself to leave this glade. I have spent so long searching for my sons that I find it hard to leave them, even if they are...

One day. That is all we had together.

They had not lived even three years and they were taken. They had not the opportunity to see the land of their ancestors. It is my fault. I should have sent them to Jötunheim with their mother when they were born. They would have grown large and menacing. Hyrrokkin would have raised them properly, not under the oppression of the Æsir. They stayed in Asgard for me, just as my family stayed in Asgard for Loki. This is because of me. Kára's tragedy happened because of me. Balder's death happened because of me. And now my

PETER CURSON

sons.

    I am not sure if it is my rationale or my instincts telling me, but it is time for me to leave; I cannot stay here forever. But where do I now go? This is the question I asked myself for the time after I reunited with my sons. It seemed like an easier question then. But now that I am alone, it is unanswerable. I truly am alone. There is no one in this world. My wife is not here. My brother has forsaken me. And now my sons... It is senseless, but it seems like abandonment leaving my sons here and continuing on with my life. Should it not be the other way around—that they continue through life while I am the one to perish first? Oh, Sköll and Hati, please forgive me. Wherever you now are, forgive—

    How foolish am I! Grief indeed is a cloak and despair a bottomless pit. I know where my sons now are—I have been there before. Hélheim. I went to retrieve Balder from the Land of the Dead, though Hél did not give him back breath and a beating heart. Yet he was an Ás and it was by the hands of the Æsir she met her unjust fate. Sköll and Hati are Jötunn. They are her brother-sons. And when she learns of the happenings in my life since last we spoke, she will not hold me in contempt any longer. Surely she will lend me her aid. There is hope for you still, my sons, and I will continue to fight for the day where we are reunited in life.

    So, with a deep breath, I raise myself from the ground, but before I leave, I walk to where my sons now rest. I lower my head, close my eyes, and breathe in, finding each their scent. I hold it within my lungs for a long while, savoring it. They are my strength and I will continue on in their names. They will be saved. I exhale and open my eyes and reclaim my determination. With my sons in my heart, I leave the glade south towards the next town.

ᛗᛁᚷᚺᛏ

EIGHT

I will reach the trading town between Norvay and Svealand soon. The day passed me by along my short trek and the evening sky turns above. To my great relief, the cloudy weather turned to blue sky and warm sun, lighting my way and bringing out the wildlife. I need to rid my mouth from the taste of human flesh. A bear would do nicely right now. But I would also settle for a deer. Alas, I find two young deer and hunt them with ease. Will none of these animals offer a good hunt? I know I am large and strong and can catch any animal I please, but that does not mean I would not rather get my heart pounding and earn my kill. Ah, it matters not. What matters is my satisfied belly and that I will have the strength to continue my journey.

    The town is quiet during this late hour but there still remains some travelers in the marketplace readying themselves for a night in the wilderness. It makes me ponder what business presses them onwards into the dark of night. Do they have a lord who they return to with all haste? Or are they believers of the *Varulv* who are looking to escape these lands?

PETER CURSON

When will the Norsemen discover Hämnd's doom, I wonder. I left none alive. None escaped. Perhaps a traveler will venture north and see the town destroyed and the people slaughtered. Will they believe in the *Varulv* then? Or will it be Sigurd who returns looking to find me only to discover the fate his people met after he deserted them? Either outcome is fine by me.

    I shifted to my normal form well away from this town so as not to be seen. The travelers pay me little attention while innkeepers attempt to sell me a room for the night. At first, I am reluctant for I am set to purpose. But as the world darkens, my rationale sets in for I will not find anyone who can help at night. So I walk back and find an inn with a roaring fire and many people inside. The men are drunk and the few women are as well. The wenches are frustrated for their guests frequently shout, make advances, and handle them. It appears that I will not find help in here. With a plate of meat and bread and a mug of ale, I plant myself at a small table with my back to the wall and wait out the night.

    The humans are relentless with their drinking and shouting. I now see that the Einherjar do not become this way because of Valhalla, they were already this way. At least the Norsemen are. Valhalla is simply their eternal place of food, drink, and merriment. If their naïve human minds were not so easily blinded, they would see the Æsir for the cruel oppressors they really are. But I do not blame them. Pleasures of the body and mind easily ensnare the humans and so when Odin rewards them with such pleasures, it is the blind leading the blind.

    The women manage to pull their husbands away and guide them to their beds, but most of the men remain despite the late hour. Do they not have fields to tend to in the morning? Or smithies to run? Surely they would not wish to hear the clanging of hammer on metal with a sickness over their drunken heads.

LEGEND OF FENRIR

The door swings open and in walks a cloaked man with hood over his head, covering his face. A skittish man he is, carrying a sack over his shoulder with a drum and a small leather pouch tied to his belt. Something weighs heavily on his mind. He makes his way through the room, finding a spot in the corner away from the others. Hunching himself over the table, he grabs his small pouch and empties its contents upon the table, rattling as they do. Though I cannot see what the contents are. He shakes his head in confusion, grabs the items, drops them on the table again, and shakes his head some more. Curious, I rise and amble across the room until I can see his table. He stares at a set of small bones, cut and shaped into flat circles. The torch flames flicker revealing that the bone pieces are each inscribed with their own unique marking, some of which I recognize instantly. Along with several others, I see the same markings that were on Sigurd's sword. If those markings were indeed the source of its power, I must speak with this man to understand what the markings are.

I approach the man and set a mug of ale on the table, startling him.

"May I join you?" I ask.

He seems hesitant, and does not look me in the eye, instead he slowly rounds up his bone pieces as one would to not cause alarm. "Why?"

"I have a couple questions I need answered."

"What makes you think I have those answers?" He keeps his face hidden from me, revealing only a thinning gray beard.

"One of my questions deals with the markings you play with."

His head twitches and after a moment's ponder, he motions for me to sit, taking a drink from the mug I offered. I sit on the chair opposite him and still he keeps his head lowered, hidden by the shadow of his hood. I sense no malice from his demeanor. He is not nervous because of me nor is he afraid. His voice, raspy and slow, shows his age. All I can discover about this man is that he is simply confused.

"How do you know of them?" he asks not taking his eyes off the markings.

"I have seen them recently. They were etched into the blade of a sword, but only some of them. This sword... it was a magicked blade." He raised his head at once, revealing a wrinkled face and defeated eyes begging me to continue. "The sword, bearing a pulsating red glow, held a hidden power within it that could send a bear flying through the air if struck. From what my eyes could see, the markings were the source of its power."

"Show me," he says pushing me all of his pieces. "Show me the markings."

I look hard at all the pieces searching my memory for the right ones. One by one, I picked them out and laid them before him.

"Othala, Thurisaz, Uruz, yes, yes. Powerful indeed. Very powerful."

"What are they? What do they mean?"

"They are runes."

Runes. I have heard a tale of these magical symbols before. The Three Norns. They are masters of destiny and fate who sit underneath Yggdrasil and control the fates of the worlds by carving runes onto its trunk. How did I not think of this sooner?

"As for what they all mean," he continues, "I wish I could recall. I learned of them from King Alf's own shaman. There stands a small group of us in Svealand who practice shamanism."

"*Seid* magic?" I ask.

He laughs. "No, that is far beyond my power—perhaps with the help of the runes one day. King Alf's shaman

LEGEND OF FENRIR

may be able to practice *seid* magic and change the course of destiny, but not the rest of us."

"Where did he learn of these runes?"

"He would not say. Only the King knows. All they would say is that they were "given" the runes. By whom, I do not know and could not speculate an answer."

"If you do not practice *seid* magic, what is it you do practice?"

"What my brethren and I do is see through this world around us, past it, and to the World Tree beyond."

"You can see the other eight worlds?"

"Sometimes. It is not as simple as opening your eyes and looking to the fields of Asgard or the forests of Alfheim."

"What about Hélheim?"

He looks at me sternly. "Why would I look into a place such as that? What is your business with any of this?"

"Like I said, I just had a couple of questions."

"Your first question has led to an irritating string of others but nonetheless I will ask: what is your second question?"

"You have already answered it," I say and I grab him by the hair and slam his head against the table, knocking him unconscious. I gather up his rune pieces, put them in their pouch, and lift the shaman over my shoulder, carrying him out of the inn, making him out to be a drunkard, and bring him to the forest beyond the town.

After a few hours, I slap the shaman awake. Night is at its darkest and it takes his eyes a few moments to adjust. He goes to hold his painful head and finds that I have tied his hands behind his back. Looking around, he sees the small clearing in the forest I have found for us. He kneels in the center of four torches placed around the clearing creating a square and on the ground in front of him are his small pouch, drum, and sack. I kneel down beside him and open the sack,

86

PETER CURSON

rifling through it. First, I find some bread and toss it aside. Next, a small bottle with what smells like poorly made wine. I keep it for now. I then pull out a bundle of leaves tied with a string. Unwrapping it, I find inside the leaves a few strands of odd-smelling herbs and a handful of mushrooms. Last, I remove a mortar and pestle.

"You have testified that you can traverse Midgard's boundaries and see the other worlds. I will need you to send me instead, but this time it will be different. You will send me in my entirety from the lands of this world and set my feet upon the plains of Hélheim."

"Are you cracked?" My facial expression answers his question. "It is folly. Not only are you mad for wishing to go to such a place, I have only been able to see past Midgard. I cannot send your body."

"You can with these," I say dropping the pouch of runes in front of him. "They contain unimaginable power, the likes of which you cannot comprehend. They have the power to bring down mighty beasts that the gods themselves would not have been able to best. Use them. Do what you must. Send me to Hélheim."

He looks down at his pouch, certainly contemplating whether it is possible or not do accomplish this feat. In truth, I do not hold much faith in him. Yet that will not stop me. He will try and try again until I either depart from this world or he proves his uselessness.

"I will try. It appears I have no choice in the matter. Yet one problem remains: if I am successful, I will not be able to bring you back."

"You need not worry about that. Worry now about how you will get me there—and do not attempt to bring me any harm, for you will not enjoy the outcome nearly as much as me."

"You need not worry. I will not bring you any harm

LEGEND OF FENRIR

because sending you to Hélheim would deliver me from your hands all the same."

I nod and untie his hands. After rolling his shoulders and stretching his arms, he first reaches for the herbs and mushrooms. After crushing and mixing them in his mortar, he mixes them with the wine and takes a drink. He then hands it to me. I sniff. Putrid. Yet, he himself had willingly taken the first drink. So shall I.

Next, he snatches his runes and dumps them in the dirt, separating and turning them until they all face up towards the moon. He begins to make piles. Some he places in a pile quickly, others he thinks about for long moments at a time before making his decisions.

"Explain to me what you are doing," I say.

"Each rune is different, holding different power and properties. These ones here we will not need for they hold power pertaining to fertility, wealth, and whatnot. These ones here we need without any doubt. Allow me to ponder on the remaining runes, for I must work to remember their meanings and powers."

"How can you forget such things?"

"Runes are complex. It is not enough to say this rune is just about strength. It also represents victory, and possibly a handful of other related, but different, forces."

This sounds familiar. But whatever hunches I have must wait. All my focus must be trained on the situation before me, which seems to grow harder with each passing second. My vision seems to blur at times, or darken. The ground before me even seems to move if I stare at it long enough as though a tunnel has formed in the dirt falling away into an abyss of nothingness.

I shake my head and my vision returns almost to normal. I look back up to the shaman who ponders the last rune in his selection, and decides to put it aside. Now only six runes remain before him:

ᛖᚱᚨᚲᛊᛇ

"What do they mean?"

"Ehwaz and Raido, transportation and journey, for that is what you set upon. Ansuz and Kenaz, insight and revelation, for that is what I will need. Sowilo and Perthro, success and mystery, for added chance of success in this uncertain task."

He says their names and meanings with enough confidence to assuage as much doubt as can be expected. Rising to his feet with the six runes in hand, he approaches me in the center of the torches and tells me to hold out my hands palms up. I do so. He places four of the runes in one hand and the remaining two in my other. Swooping down, he picks up his drum and stands opposite me. "I will now begin."

The shaman closes his eyes and his face hardens in concentration. His breathing remains calm and deliberate, calm yet purposeful. No wind blows tonight leaving a warm and silent night, save for the soft sound of the torches surrounding us. He strikes his drum, a low and soft sound. The reverberations course through my body, lingering a while deep within my ears. He strikes again, this time louder. Then a few sharp beats. Soon, a rhythm forms. I feel each vibration flow through me, and they rattle me to my core. My head starts to whirl and my vision with it, going slower than my eyes move.

"Close your eyes," he says. I do so. "Control your breathing. Slowly. Inhale with me, exhale with me." He beats upon the drum three more times to conclude his rhythm and places the drum on the ground. His hands clasp on top of

LEGEND OF FENRIR

mine. They are cold and dry, large and rough. Surely this man was a warrior in his younger days, perhaps a Viking, one of the raiding seafarers. Surely there is no other way for a man's hands to become so strong and weathered if not by days at sea and at war.

"We are ready. Together we will peer beyond this world. Imagine the world slipping away beside you. The trees, the water, and the horizon beyond. Watch it slip away."

As he says these words, I remember sitting upon Odin's throne and how the world at once, like the shaman says, slipped away—and with this thought, I can see the shaman and the forest around me even with my eyes remaining closed. And just as on the throne, I imagine the world falling away, and so it did. The forest drifts away, the town, and all the world until all I see is darkness around me. Further and further into the dark I go until I break through night's hold and see before me a mighty tree. The World Tree. Yggdrasil. What a sight! This marks the third time I have laid eyes upon this cosmological sight. It must be from my time here on Midgard, but it seems even greater and more majestic than it used to. While living in Asgard, I was accustomed to wondrous sights that the humans would deem ethereal. It is truly a heart-lifting sight. Having just left Midgard, we near halfway down Yggdrasil's trunk. Above soar innumerable branches stretching far into the gaping abyss with leaves that could cover entire countries on Midgard's world. Though I am far away, I can see nestled in the boughs some of the other worlds. Alfheim, a green and luscious world. Vanaheim, also green but otherworldly in itself—less bright and somehow less tame. And there is Asgard, the pinnacle of strength and beauty—as I yet know. Would I behold Jötunheim for the first time with my own two eyes, I surely would change my mind. Unfortunately, I cannot journey there. Not without my sons. I will not return to Hyrrokkin and tell her our sons are lost to us unless I do all

PETER CURSON

in my power to bring them with me.

I bring my gaze from the top of the tree, scanning it for a peculiar creature, but I cannot find it. I listen for the pitter patter of its feet, the scratching and scurrying, but it does not reveal itself. What a shame. I would have liked to lay eyes upon Ratatosk the giant squirrel again without fear of being consumed by it. Perhaps he is at the top of Yggdrasil where the Great Eagle makes its nest, or under the deepest root where the dragon Nidhogg resides. Ratatosk spends his days perpetuating harmful remarks between the eagle and dragon, furthering their never-ending hatred of the other. What an existence they have.

Yet as I look around for the squirrel, something is amiss. I sniff. Nothing. I do not smell the tree. Yggdrasil's aroma is something I will never in this life forget but it is lost to me. I am not here; I merely see.

The shaman goes to speak but I am already ahead of him. I look down and see far away Yggdrasil's roots. My vision rushes there with incredible speed until I drift through the vast entanglement. And soon, I see it. A world of utter darkness and an ever-deepening fog. The World of the Dead. Hélheim.

"You have been here before," the shaman says with fear gripping his voice.

"Yes, what seems like many years ago."

"I will not ask why for I fear the answer and wish to keep our concentration fixed upon this world. Alright, now comes the final part. Gaze out to Hélheim. Look deep into the mist. Penetrate the darkness. Bring from your memories a single place in that world. Concentrate hard on it. Visualize that place: all its surroundings, sights, and smells."

As I construct the place from memory, I feel something flow through me. Something powerful. A force stronger than instinct. It wraps around my body engulfing me. I fight it. It is not natural. It is beyond me. But the vision before me

LEGEND OF FENRIR

begins to slip. And this is when I realize that it is the power of the runes and that they are working with me. At once, I relinquish myself to the power of the runes and think hard on my vision one last time. And I fall.

A floor of stone catches me. It is cold—deathly cold. I open my eyes and see my hand in front of me, palm against blackened stone. I am no longer in a vision and I am no longer in the forest. Walls surround me covered with banners and the hanging corpses of mutilated beasts. From the windows pour in a ghastly light and a stench more foul than any other. I made it. I am in the very throne room of Hél's castle. Within seconds I hear something big rushing towards me and I know at once what it is. I push myself off the ground, shifting as I do so, and am immediately tackled by a large creature. It lands on top of me and I snap my jaws, clamping down on the beast above me. I roll over, sinking in my teeth, tasting foul blood. Claws scratch at my underbelly and I release, distancing myself. I recover my stance and see before me a hound nearly my equal. He bleeds from his neck and I snicker: it is where I bit him last time. Garm is his name and he is my sister's hound.

I growl deep. He knows I can best him. Of course, that would not stop him from protecting his master or his world. But he takes a moment to sniff my scent and recognizes me. I am his master's family and he will not bring me to harm. A shock indeed it must have been to see a man appear from nothing right in front of him. I gaze around the room properly and see that we are alone. Garm steps away from me and walks out of the room onto the balcony that overlooks an expansive field covered with thousands upon thousands of the living-dead fighting one another in an endless struggle that cannot be won. Garm plants himself and howls as best as a dead hound can. It is not clear and profound, but cackled and void of vigor. Death is riddled in its howl and though I despise this hound for what he is, I cannot help but pity him. A spiteful

PETER CURSON

beast he is, but a canine nonetheless.

    I shift back to my normal self and step out upon the balcony. Across the cursed plains and amidst the fury of battle, I see a figure riding upon a black horse. It does not take her darkened skin or even the flames encircling her arms to know that it is Hél. When last I saw her, she did not recognize me at first glance——and that was not long after she was slain by the hands of Odin. It has now been years since the day I departed these lands and I do not know what to expect.

    Hél rides hard across the plains until she is at the foot of the castle and she launches herself off her horse and soars to the top of her castle, landing in front of me. The fires around her arms intensify and her skin turns even darker. Yet I am still drawn to her eyes: orange with a heat unquenchable. In her hand, she grips her whip, ready to strike.

    I wait for her to speak first but she keeps her lips sealed and the silence bears down upon me. "Sister."

    "Fenrir." She remembers me.

    "Surely you know why I am here."

    After a labored breath, she mutters "I do," and brushes past me into her throne. I re-enter the throne room with Garm at my back. She continues. "Ever since you left on your mission for Balder's resurrection, I have kept my ears open for any news of you. Imagine my surprise when you defy the gods and escape to Midgard. Shortly thereafter, humans flood through my world mauled and slain by a giant wolf. Many more by two giant wolves. You and your sons have been busy. And could you imagine my surprise next when your very sons arrive at my gate?"

    "Where are they?"

    "They are dead, Fenrir, like everything else in this world. Did your experience with Balder teach you nothing? The dead will forever remain so."

    "You have the power to send them back," I say. "You

LEGEND OF FENRIR

would have resurrected Balder if Loki did not deceive us all. You would have restored life to an Ás. Surely you will not turn your back on fellow Jötnar—on your brother-sons. I did anything and everything I could to find my sons. That is evident by my presence before you."

"What would you do with your sons returned to you?"

"We would return to Jötunheim, where their mother waits and where our army rises. The Jötnar prepare for the greatest war in our history; they set out to destroy the Æsir. I would be a part of that battle. And so would my sons if their hearts still beat in their chests."

She scoffs. "You are damned, Fenrir. Wretched and damned."

"Does this news not delight you? Now it is you who have forgotten our last meeting. You told me to never return unless I wish to destroy the Æsir once and for all. I do. I want them all to perish for what they have done. For what they have done to us. Do you not wish this?"

"It does delight me! It awakens my cold, dead heart. What enrages me is you! You would raise your sons from the dead only to send them back? A father would shield his sons from such a fate. What happened to you? You are no better than Loki."

No. She is wrong. I am not Loki. I have made mistakes; this I know. I should have sent them far from the gods when they were born. I should have died for them.

But is there some truth in her words? Surely they would fight alongside the Jötnar if they were alive. And as evidenced by the power of the runes, many will die in this war. I would give them the chance to enact revenge on the gods who wronged them, as I one day will, but would I bring them back to the torment of war?

"Even if I am to bring them back only to enter the suffering of war, is it not better than remaining here among the dead for the rest of eternity? Is it not better to fight with hope than to not have any hope at all?"

"I am sure that is how Loki rationalized our punishments: keeping the Jötunn hope alive. Will you too sacrifice your sons to that end?"

I break myself from her gaze for her words churn my insides. My mind cannot find an answer. I walk back onto the balcony from where I can see the dead soldiers brawling one another in a pathetic battle without heroes, yet it gives me the stimulus I need to drown out all other thoughts and let my innermost mind sort out my feelings. If my sons were to be resurrected, surely I would not be able to hold them back from enacting revenge on Sigurd. Further yet, I could not stop them from joining their kind in the war against the Æsir for what they have done. I would not be able to shield them from war and from danger. If I was to make this decision even a fortnight ago, it would be an easy one. I thought me and my sons undefeatable. A pack of three without equal. Yet the deeds of one human with a magicked blade proved me utterly wrong. And if they were to be resurrected and the worst was to happen during the war… How could a father even allow the opportunity for his sons to die two deaths? How could I watch them die twice?

Hél approaches. "Come with me."

She leads me back into the castle to a narrow staircase that winds its way upwards. Brittle torches of dead wood burn an eternal purple flame, lighting the staircase and at the top she opens a door leading to the roof of her castle. I step out and see them. Sköll and Hati. They are statues, still and gray, turned to stone, immobilized in positions of attack and mid-howl. I run to them and place my hands on their cold, stone bodies. Their scents are lost and if it was not for the intricate detail and the unique expressions on their faces that I recognize, I would not believe these statues to really be my sons.

LEGEND OF FENRIR

"What have you done to them?"

"Nothing of any harm. When they arrived, I saw death consuming them as it does all beings as they cross the fog to the river Gjöll. Yet they were resilient and when they reached the river guardian Modgud, they still yet clung to the last scraps of themselves. And so I turned them into stone to immortalize their personalities——that they may never lose themselves completely in this desolate world bereft of life."

I lay my head on Hati's leg and cannot keep back my tears. My sons. My sons...

"Whatever you may now think of me, brother, I have not lost all sense of compassion. I know of your sons' stories, as I do all who pass through the fog into my domain. They did not deserve the punishment Odin enacted. Even less so than we did. The choice is yours, Fenrir."

What I would give to see them full of life once more. I look at my sons' faces and when I do, my heart falls in my chest and I know my decision.

"I cannot take them back with me. Though they deserve a full life, they do not deserve to be brought back to further death and tragedy. Though they deserve to gain vengeance on those who wronged them, it now rests on my shoulders to see it done. Hél, you have saved them from the lifeless existence of this world. For that I am thankful. And ultimately, that has stayed my decision to revive them. Here, they are safe and within these casts of stone, they are themselves."

Hél gazes into my watery eyes and closes her own, then nods. "I see your tormented soul. I see the pain of letting your sons go. It moves my heart. There is something yet I will do for Sköll and Hati. I release them from death but not restore them to life in the Nine Worlds. When they arrived here, all that remained in their minds were their last thoughts on Earth: the sun and the moon. That is where I will send them, into the cosmos surrounding the World Tree so that they can be at peace with that which they love and without fear of any worldly pain."

I look at Hél and for the first time since I arrived, I find my old sister behind her dark and powerful form. I move to her without hesitation and embrace her tight. She stirs but she does not wrap her arms around me. Yet, her dark hair flutters and turns gold, just for a moment before turning back, but for that moment, she was my sister in her normal self.

"Come," she says, "I will send them now. If you would wish it, I can wake them from their stone slumbers here so that you could have a moment with them to say a last farewell."

I nod. Hél motions me on and I turn back to face my sons. And I shift. If a moment is all I have, we will spend it as we are meant to. Before I can take another breath, the grayness of their stone bodies both darken and soften until their chiseled appearance fades almost completely and in a blink of an eye, Sköll and Hati are freed from their immobile prison. Their dark fur gleams the twilit sky but their eyes regain only some of their color for they have begun to turn a milky white.

They see me and before I can react, they pounce on top of me and hug me tightly between their paws, nuzzling themselves within my fur. My legs give in and we fall to the ground together but do not let go. Not yet. Not just yet. I close my eyes and all else fades away. My sons' heat warms me in the midst of a cold world. Their heartbeats pound against me while surrounded by this lifeless void. Their tails wag. Oh, my sons. You make me happy. So truly happy.

And just as soon as they came to life, I open my eyes and find my sons are gone, passed on from even the World of the Dead to the cosmos where I am sure they will spend their days chasing after the sun and moon as they would chase their own tails. Farewell Sköll and Hati. Farewell my sons.

NINE

After re-entering the castle, Hél feeds Garm a flank of rotting meat and sits upon her throne. I am starting to become accustomed to her new disposition. She remains silent unless otherwise engaged, never starting any conversation on her own. She smiles not nor shows any other outward signs of emotion. Joy, sadness, anger, confusion, they are all absent, which makes it very hard to read her despite being my sister. But, as been proven, there remains emotion under her grim façade, even if only a pittance. The only tell I can find is from her posture, which shows determination. She is set to some purpose. She first asks me about how I traveled to her world. I tell her it was by the powers of a shaman but ultimately it was the work of the runes—of which she has already heard. She keeps quiet for a moment to contemplate, then finds her tongue.

"You told me you are ready to fight against the Æsir," she says, "and that the Jötnar are raising an army to do just that?"

"Yes. The Jötnar army has grown for many, many

PETER CURSON

years now, but only within the past few have they set their minds to purpose to besiege and destroy Asgard. From last I heard from my wife, one of Jötunheim's leaders in this war, they were close to achieving the ranks needed at the time I escaped Asgard. I am sure now, two years later, that they are prepared."

"You are wrong. It is true that the Jötnar have the numbers to wage war against the Æsir, however, Odin has the advantage."

"How do you mean?"

"The runes of which you spoke, did the shaman tell you from where they come?"

"From King Alf's shaman. How he came by them, I do not know."

"They were not discovered by him or by any other human. It was Odin who discovered them and Odin who handed them down to the King."

"I spent a long time in Asgard and only once did I hear mention of the runes and that was in regard to the Three Norns. The Æsir do not know them."

"That was true. Odin discovered them recently, shortly after his ravens returned to him bearing news of your intentions to find your sons. From my understanding, he thought long and hard on how he could stop you, for if you joined with your sons, you would run rampant on Midgard and the humans would be powerless to stand against you. Is that not why he kept you in Asgard instead of banishing you like Jor and I? He realized it would not be through sheer force of arms that you and your sons would be brought down, but by something unprecedented. Yet through all his wisdom, he could not find what he sought. He needed more knowledge. A sacrifice was needed. We know he sacrificed his right eye in order to gain the wisdom from Mímir's Well. Now he went further. In a feat I do not fully understand, Odin sacrificed

LEGEND OF FENRIR

himself—to himself."

Now I know nothing of sacrifices and rituals, but that makes no sense to my mind. How can someone sacrifice himself to himself? Hél reads my confusion, shared within her own mind, but she continues telling this story for it is all she can do.

"He hung himself from the very branches of Yggdrasil and pierced himself with Gungnir, his spear. Yet, he did not die. Not fully. He hung upon those branches foregoing food and water for nine days and nine nights. His body was broken and his will diminished. Neither was he fully alive nor was he dead. I know of this because I could feel his overwhelming presence. His death was nigh at hand, and I awaited him with all intention of destroying him a hundred times over when he landed in my realm before unleashing my hordes upon him. Yet on that ninth night, his head lost its strength. With chin to chest, all he could do was stare down Yggdrasil's trunk, and there he could see from where it sprouts: Urd's Well, where the Three Norns reside, endlessly carving their patterns on the tree. The runes. He stared ever on into the well and before the tenth sun shone upon him, I saw his face awaken with revelation. He understood. With an excruciating scream, he removed himself from the tree and made all haste to Midgard, regaining his lifeforce with each step until I could no longer sense him."

That is indeed an extraordinary tale, one I would not believe if it were not for Hél's accurate depiction and the look of recollection in her eyes. That must be it. Odin discovered the runes and unveiled their secrets, then making his way to Midgard to pass along his knowledge to King Alf and his shaman. And to Sigurd. This realization enrages the fire within me and I cannot control it. Odin's actions led to my sons' deaths. He will die by my jaws for what he has done. But first, I must avenge my sons. Sigurd, you are next.

PETER CURSON

"It is time for me to fight, sister. Jötunheim prepares for war, so too should Hélheim. I would return to Jötunheim to lead the armies alongside their leaders, but first I must kill Sigurd. I cannot let his actions go unanswered. Send me to Midgard once more so that I may avenge Sköll and Hati. Thereafter I will go to our homeland. Then together, I at the head of the Jötnar and you leading your army of the dead, we will storm Asgard with all our strength and watch it crumble."

"If that is what you wish, I will support your desire for revenge. With knowledge of the runes, the Æsir stand more powerful than we can imagine. In your absence, I will send word to Jötunheim to prepare accordingly and upon your return, we will be ready. Yet do not underestimate Sigurd for even without his enchanted blade, he is a formidable foe. Even now, being hailed as the slayer of the *Varulv*s, he has been tasked with slaying a new monster who has beset their lands: Fafnir the dragon."

A dragon? Surely she is not serious. I have heard the word dragon mentioned only once on Midgard and it was from that cracked fool in Birca. Wait, there was also that Norseman who I met before traveling to Birca. In any regard, she continues to tell me that Fafnir was not born a dragon, but a dwarf. As the son of the dwarven King Hreidmar, he was already someone to be reckoned with. Yet, as all dwarves, he had a weakness to anything with a shine and luster. His father kept a vast hoard of gold in his underground castle on Nidavellir that Fafnir guarded. And with each passing day, the wealth consumed his heart. But it was not until an incident with the Æsir that he acted upon his desires.

"It was Odin, Hoenir, and Loki who began the spiral of events that led to this day," Hél says. "Years ago on their travels through Nidavellir, they came across a large otter, one that could alone feed a host of people. So they killed it and skinned it, then made their way to King Hreidmar's castle.

LEGEND OF FENRIR

However, Fafnir was not Hreidmar's only son. Of his other sons, there is one named Otr, named for his shapeshifting ability. He was the otter Odin, Hoenir, and our father killed. And upon hearing this tale, the dwarf king captured Odin and Hoenir, telling Loki that to release them, he would have to pay a ransom of gold that would fit inside the hide of his dead son. And so Loki traveled across the World of the Dwarves and came upon a waterfall fed pool in which swam a lone fish, larger than any other he had seen. Not wishing to be deceived twice, he caught the fish and found it to be another dwarf. Loki forced the dwarf to reveal his hoard, including the prized gold ring named Andvaranaut. As Loki left to pay the ransom, the dwarf cursed all the gold in his hoard so that it would bring ruin to any who kept it.

"Loki paid the ransom and returned to Asgard with Odin and Hoenir. The King added the ransomed gold to his horde and it consumed Fafnir. Every day thereafter, Fafnir sought after the gold, coveting it above even the brightest jewels, and the curse poisoned his heart and mind, driving him mad. So much so that one day he slayed his father the king and stole away the gold so that it would remain his forever. A traitor and criminal to his people, he took the hoard to Midgard and hid away in the far northern forests of Svealand where no one would find him and for years the curse has poisoned him until he could not stave it off any longer. The curse destroyed his body, skin and bone, and reformed him into a mighty dragon."

I cannot help but grunt a hollow laugh. Of course it would be both Odin and Loki who caused such a thing to happen. It is just like Loki to ignore warnings of curses and cast them about in the wind so long as the consequences do not land on him. And would Odin not correct this wrong after seeing what he has caused? No, for he is a treacherous cretin without any honor or integrity, or any other such virtue. "It truly seems that Odin does not care for the humans. He sends Jormungand to terrorize their seas, Sköll and Hati to terrorize their lands, and is the cause for a dragon that threatens the Norsemen. Pah. It matters not. If Sigurd sets out to slay Fafnir, that is where I will find him."

"Very well. Tread carefully, Fenrir, for Sigurd has already proven himself and Fafnir may yet as well. When you are ready, I will send you back to Svealand to the outskirts of Fafnir's territory."

"Before you do," I say, a little hesitant with my next words. "Where is Balder? What has become of him?"

Her constant apathetic expression shows that she is not surprised by my question yet she waits a moment. Perhaps she wonders if she should tell me, which would mean something unfortunate. I see her jaw loosen and she exhales as one would when tired of conversation. "When his wife Nanna arrived into my lands, I brought her here to her husband and the moment Balder saw her, he glowed. And so did she, a radiant and pure light like that on a chilled winter day after a dark and terrible storm. They held each other in a long, loving embrace I thought impossible in this world. In that moment, I understood what you saw in him. His gentle heart is one I no longer doubted. Though fierce warrior he once was, he was... different than the other Æsir gods. Truly I believed he was loved by all who knew him, even if only by name. And further, I believed he did not deserve the death he was dealt. Thus, I sent him and his wife to the furthest corner of this world where no dead soul would wander so that they could spend their eternity together, sheltered from death and misery as best as can be done in my world."

Joyous news. Joyous indeed. That she showed them mercy despite her hatred, it gladdens my heart. If time had been more generous, I would seek them out. Would they even remember me; have they lost their minds as all dead people

LEGEND OF FENRIR

do? Or would it be a candid reunion of friends long since removed? My mind rests on the fact that despite everything that has happened and that which remains unsettled, Balder and Nanna are together. Hél has shown great compassion. Yet, my mind wanders. If only she showed such compassion when I first pleaded for Balder's life, perhaps the events of the past few years could have been avoided. He would have lived once again beside me. Týr and Balder would have remained my friends and I would have advanced in higher regards in the eyes of the Æsir, perhaps to see the day where Odin would release me from the bonds of his judgement, then inevitably to Jötunheim thereafter. Although, if she relinquished Balder to me, there would never have been a funeral and I would never have met Hyrrokkin nor had Sköll and Hati as sons. As terrible as the misfortunes have been since that day Balder was slain, I would not have a life without Sköll and Hati. The joy they have brought me, the pride that swells in my heart, the memories I will forever hold close to my breast, I would not trade them for anything. Now, I must fight to bring justice to those behind their deaths. With a deep inhale and sharp exhale, I nod. And before I know it, Hél, her hound, and her castle disappear in a black fog.

TEN

I arrive in Midgard to a place I have not seen before; I would have remembered if I did. Before me stretches what would have once been called a forest. Shreds of brown leaves cover the ground, blown this way and that by the wind. Dried, withered trees dot the landscape amidst bushes long since drained of life. The trees, dead for many years, used to be evergreen—never losing their green needles even through the harshest of winters. Yet the needles have fallen off these trees and none remain, leaving their hosts naked: gray with bark rotted and peeling. They stand as parched skeletons contrasting the life the forest once held with the death now tormenting it. This is unnatural. And it goes on for miles northward until distant mountains stop and contain the disease. I look behind me and find that the land regains its color quickly, and I recognize that this indeed is Svealand. What has come to pass here that would destroy the land so? This is a fell deed. To tarnish and poison nature like this deserves nothing but a painful death.

    I would remain directionless if not for a dense wood in the distance with a river running through its center. The

LEGEND OF FENRIR

trees there yet cling to life, bearing needles and leaves, but they stand equally cursed in fate. I would not wish any animal to roam there nor any bird to make its nest. But as the only piece of land not marred by death and decay, it remains the only place for a dragon to make its home in this forsaken place. I shift and begin on my way.

  The smells of this area meet my nose. For a land poisoned by such unnatural means, it does not reek. The trees smell as any withered tree would. The soil remains firm and otherwise normal. What caused this then? Perhaps when the Svear learned of Fafnir, and failed when they came to slay him, they decided to burn him within the forest. Or perhaps it was by Fafnir's flames, not by human torches, that incinerated the forest. Yet fire could not have brought the end to this forest for the trees left standing would have no bark instead of rotted bark and would stand black, scorched to their cores. Nay. It seems I must attribute this to the curse that lies upon the dragon himself. In fact, I hope such is the case—I would rather Fafnir prove a flameless dragon. Though, with my luck, he will have ten heads and shoot flames out his ass.

  Gazing across the plains of toxicity, I see no signs of life. No critters. No birds or vultures. Not even any bugs in the dirt. But more disappointingly, no Sigurd. If luck would grace me, I would find him and kill him before coming any nearer to the dragon. I care not for Fafnir nor his curse nor the humans he may terrorize. He is only a piece on this gameboard whose only use is to entrap my enemy. Is this the best strategy? By all means no, but if there are any others, they elude my mind. Although, it would be feasible to find King Alf's abode and wait in hiding until Sigurd arrives. However, my battle with him will be hard-fought as it is without the King's armies within arm's reach. In any regard, Fafnir may actually have some uses besides bait. With proper maneuvering, I could use him as an obstacle or as a way to tire my enemy. A fair fight? No. But if Sigurd has Odin on his side, why should I not have a dragon? All shall unfold soon enough. But whatever I do, I cannot make myself an enemy of Fafnir for even I with all my strength and size would not match a dragon alone.

    I near the slowly-decaying forest in the center of this wasteland by evening's arrival, which worries me. A night alone in this forest deprived of foliage means I will remain vulnerable, with only the dark of night to conceal me. The forest is not large either; a human could cross from one end to the other within nearly a day. But it is large enough to comfortably hide a dragon. I must make it there before darkness fully sets about the world lest I find myself without a place in which to hide for the night.

    Sleep is greatly needed. I have not slept for... well, an unknown amount of days. Time does not move in Hélheim as it does in Asgard or Midgard. My drooping eyelids feel as though I spent only one day there, meaning two nights without sleep. If I am to battle Sigurd, I will need a full rest to rejuvenate body and mind. Though, my stomach will remain empty for even if there are animals in this forest nearly before me, they will more than likely prove toxic like the rest of the land.

    Alas, I arrive at the forest's edge with a dark blue sky above, quickly turning darker. Nothing I hear upon the soft breeze nor anything I smell in the air. Indeed, I do not know the scent of a dragon, but I would notice any smell foreign to my nostrils. None fill the air, not even a whiff. As I would have guessed, Fafnir makes his home in the heart of the forest. It only makes sense to hoard one's stockpile in the hardest place to find and easiest place to protect, not on the edge of a wasteland readily traversed. Only a short way to go yet. I enter the forest.

LEGEND OF FENRIR

Never would I have thought entering a forest would fill me with such grief and despair. Where is the calmness and tranquility? Where is the beauty in this? This forest has been robbed of such life and majesty that all nature holds—that intrinsic spirit. Now all that remains is a void that mocks all of creation and all things that grow.

Night advances upon the world quickly, darkening the trees around me so that they hide their grievous existence from my sight. Before much longer, I come across a cluster of trees reminiscent of willows. Perhaps they were one day before Fafnir and his cursed gold happened upon this place. Now they stand but as shadows in the dark, naked and breathless. Yet, they are dense with many branches and will hide me well for the night. I brush my way into their midst and under the dead sky, I fall into a shallow slumber under the withered trees.

A sound wakens me. I find that dawn is nigh and the forest is yet dim. Looking around, I see nothing noticeable or out of the ordinary. I may have to move because as the forest brightens, these small willows will not conceal me any longer. But for now, I perk my ears and listen again for the noise. Faintly, I hear it off to my left, northward, moving towards the center of the forest. Before I lose it between the trees, I pick out the cling and clang of metal. A mail shirt. Sigurd. Though, there remains only one sound making its way to my ears. He comes alone to battle the dragon? A fool he is.

Rising slowly, I peer northward but see nothing. The ground rises and falls in slow slopes preventing far field of sight. Checking my surroundings again and seeing nothing else of alarm, I silently roam through the forest. The dried needles keep my paws from making noise, but how they prickle me. I take care not to brush against any bushes nor step on any twigs and branches for a single snap may undo me. It worries me not. I have stalked my way through many a forest without

PETER CURSON

noise in search of easier game. Now my mind is set to purpose and no mistakes will I make.

In a matter of minutes, I come across a path through the forest leading the way I travel. With small ridges hugging each side of the path, it remains wide enough for horse and cart to travel upon. What remains further north of this forest that the Norsemen would have carved a path to travel? Perhaps in the days before Fafnir, there was, or still remains, a village or two in the northern regions of Svealand. In fact, I do not know how much further the lands stretch north. Perhaps there is another nation up there as large, if not larger, than Svealand and Gautland. Though, I doubt any great nations would willingly live in the harsh winters of these north lands.

Regardless of why it is here or who made it, I step down and inspect the path. As my ears earlier uncovered, only one set of horse tracks mark the path. I sniff them and my instincts flare ever so slightly. Why does the scent of this horse alarm me so? Is the scent familiar to me? I do not think so. But it is not the same horse from our last encounter. Is there anything special about it? No, it smells like horse. I inhale deeply once more and still cannot uncover what it might be. Perhaps the scent is too faint. Whatever the reason, this horse is the least of my concerns. With haste, I move along the path following the hoof prints.

The path steadily winds through the forest and after a couple of hours, I grow suspicious. Despite Sigurd riding upon horseback, I should have caught up with him by now. Could he know I stalk him and has veered off the path to catch me unawares? If he has done so, my ears do not hear the sound of his armor nor even the sound of his footfall. Would a man, even a purposed hero, travel with such haste towards a danger such as Fafnir? A fool would, one who thinks himself invincible for his recent victory against my sons. Though the only

109

LEGEND OF FENRIR

victory to which he may lay claim is that he fought me and survived—something I will soon nullify.

Picking up my pace, I continue through the forest for a while, keeping my wits about me, until I instinctively stop in my tracks. The path steadily curves but I feel a presence upon its other side. And I now know why. I hear a horse nickering. Perhaps they have stopped to eat. Could a better opportunity ever present itself? I step off the path and hide myself among the trees making no sound. With a few more steps, I see across the patch of forest and back onto the path. There he is, Sigurd standing beside his horse eating bread. His horse is turned from me, and once his back faces me also, I will attack. Five strides are all I will need to cross the forest and land upon him with unstoppable fury. Despite my stealth and soundless attack, within two strides his horse will know of me. Upon my third and fourth, Sigurd will see his horse's flinch and react. Upon my fifth, I will pounce while he reaches for his sword. Although I will land upon him with jaws open wide, he may have time to land attack before death comes to him. I have witnessed Sigurd's agility before and should not underestimate him. I must close the distance.

Against my heightened instincts, I shift to my two-legged self. It will allow me to approach without discovery since my smaller size will not give me away nor make heavy steps. Keeping low, I creep forward from tree to tree upon constant approach. Five strides in my wolf form now stands over twenty. The needles beneath me prick my feet but they cushion my footfall. They also conceal dry leaves and twigs that would surely make noise if stepped upon. Each step I choose with swift care. Fifteen steps. I close the distance. Ten steps. If I can reach but a few steps closer, I can launch myself into the air, shift, and it will be over. There is a tree nearby that will conceal me until the opportune moment arises. I step out and make for the tree.

PETER CURSON

"Sigurd!" a voice calls out.

I drop to the ground. Sigurd's attention is drawn further down the path towards the center of the forest. Another person in this cursed forest? Unlikely. He must have come with Sigurd. It matters not. This could prove beneficial since Sigurd's attention is drawn further from me. I may not get a better chance before he sets out once more. Planting my feet into the ground, I ready to shift. But something stops me: a last moment thought. What if his comrade also carries a magicked blade? I must wait. Strength alone will not destroy my foes. Not this time. Cunning and intellect will win me this fight. I position myself so that I am hidden from Sigurd's sight as well as the man who approaches. It takes until they are nearly face-to-face for me to even hear the other man in my present form. How limiting it is. Regardless, I can hear them speaking and that is what matters.

"You," Sigurd says.

"Yes, it is me. You are on the path towards Fafnir, a monster beyond all reckoning."

"Not beyond reckoning," Sigurd replies. "I have faced the two giant wolves and slayed them, even as their father fought with them."

"Indeed the three of them were fierce beasts that even the gods would struggle against, yet even I could not estimate the outcome if they had fought Fafnir. I say this to rid you of your pride of past victories for they all count for nothing against your next foe. Further yet, the reason I return to you again is to offer what aid I can."

"And I will gladly welcome it despite not knowing why you have taken such a keen interest in me and my quests."

"Does it matter my reasoning?"

"No," Sigurd says, although I can hear a hint of a lie in his voice. "It was by your aid that I achieved victory in my battle against the wolves." My eyes widen and I fight every

LEGEND OF FENRIR

urge to pounce. "You re-forged my father's sword and marked it with the magic runes, giving it immense power. Because of what you did, I was able to strike down the beasts. Without this sword, they surely would have ended me."

No, I can no longer remain hidden. The risk is no longer too great. I have to see his accomplice for now there are two men I must kill: the man who dealt the lethal strikes against my sons and the man who supplied him with the sword to do so. I shuffle from behind the tree and peer around its trunk. In front of Sigurd stands a man clothed in a tattered cloak, wearing a wide brimmed, pointy hat, and carrying a walking stick. Upon his back he carries a sack with two tall items inside His face is hidden from my sight. The rage in my heart commands my attack but my instincts bid me wait. Whoever this man may be is the source behind the runic sword. Perhaps he is the King's shaman, and if that is the case, he may prove to be an opponent with tactics I could never even conceive. They continue.

"Ah yes, it is indeed your father's sword. What do you know of it?"

"My mother told me that during the wedding celebration of Signy, my father's sister, a man came to the feast with the sword in hand and planted it firmly into a tree saying, 'He who can pull the sword from the tree is worthy of wielding it.' Everyone tried, including the greedy King of Gautland himself. But the only man who was able to wrest the sword from the tree was Sigmund, my father. It helped him win many battles during his life, but upon his last battle, he contested a man unknown to either friendly army or enemy. His opponent, fighting alone, bested my father and shattered the sword in doing so. With his dying breath, my father told my wife that she was pregnant with me and that I would one day re-forge the sword. You fulfilled his last command."

"That is not all I did. Your father's sword, its name is

PETER CURSON

Gram, and I was the one who visited the wedding upon that night and delivered the sword into your father's hand. And indeed, it was I who broke the sword upon your father's last battle."

Sigurd raises his sword against the man. "You were the one who killed my father? Why? Why would you help him then slay him? And why now would you lend me aid?" He pauses a moment. "Does this mean you will also wish to slay me?"

"Sigmund was a hero amongst heroes," the cloaked man says, remaining calm. "He led his men to victory in many battles that would have otherwise ended in decimation. But his time had come to be carried to Valhalla upon the Valkyries' wings in order to open a path to a new hero, a greater hero than even Sigmund. You."

I am done with this conversation, it means nothing to me. Sigurd, his father, this man, all of it means nothing. All that matters are their deaths by my hand. This would prove opportunity enough to attack, while their wits have escaped them. Yet, the more this man speaks, the more my instincts flare. It is so subtle that I cannot place it, but I know in my core that I must learn all I can before killing them. Patience. It is what Hél would have urged.

"Sigmund, as great as he was, would not have defeated the wolves," the man continues. "Only you could have done that, just as only you can defeat the dragon, Fafnir."

"You did not answer my last question."

"I do not know what the future holds. Even you could tell a man 'I will not kill you' one day, but then the next learn of a reason why you should. Know that this day, I stand not to oppose you, but to aid you. Focus your thoughts against the threat ahead of you, not on me."

Sigurd looks sternly at the cloaked man, surely with thoughts swimming around his mind undecipherable.

LEGEND OF FENRIR

Though, within moments, Sigurd lowers his eyes and nods. "What aid do you wish provide for my upcoming battle?"

"Aid in the form of wisdom. Alas, I have no other gift to lend. The sword has been re-forged and you have taken my prior advice and chose this steed from the King's stables who I had placed there. All I now have to give is knowledge, and possibly an extra pair of hands."

"I still do not know why you advised me to choose this horse."

The cloaked man laughs. "You will, and you will thank me for it upon a day. Now listen. Fafnir is on his way to us as we speak. We have perhaps an hour before he reaches this spot. He would not think anyone this far into his forest. Surprise is your greatest boon. When the time comes, you must make yourself as small as a mouse and strike only when victory is sure to be yours."

"I have already realized this, old man," Sigurd says.

"But you have not yet realized Fafnir's tremendous size. The father wolf may have been large to your eyes but he is a pup compared to the beast on its way. His scales prove as shields unbreakable, his claws stand as swords, his breath changing between fire and poison. The curse has created him in this way to be unconquerable so as to protect the hoard. Though, as all beings in life, he has a weakness. As all dragons, his underbelly remains unprotected, without scales——just thick hide."

"As all dragons?" Sigurd questions. "There are more?"

"Not anymore. Not in this world in any regard. Yet that is a matter for another day."

"If such a day should ever arrive. You tell me the dragon's weakness, but how can I lay attack on a dragon's underbelly?"

"How else would you but from underneath?" The cloaked man drops the sack from his shoulder and pulls out

PETER CURSON

two spades, handing one to Sigurd. They are to dig a hole so that attack may be achieved from underneath as Fafnir passes over. Perhaps this is the best chance I have. But that thought gnaws at my mind. This man is still unknown to me. Is he a shaman? A warrior? I do not know his fighting capability, and if it proves too much to handle when added alongside Sigurd, I will not leave this forest alive. No, unless I learn of who this man is and his skill, I cannot attack. Even if it means letting the man slip away for now, I must wait. Sigurd's head will be my trophy this day. And if not the cloaked man's head, that will come tomorrow.

    An hour has nearly passed since they began digging their holes. At first, it was just one in which Sigurd would lay in hiding. Then the cloaked man argued that if Sigurd opened the dragon's belly from underneath, blood would overflow the hole and drown him inside. Thus, they spent their remaining time digging holes and trenches across the whole path. The cloaked man truly is a mystery. He thinks of concepts and finds details no normal mind would ever think. Furthermore, he does not tire even from such labor. Sigurd paces his work so as to not tire himself before battle, but even he has broken into sweat. But the cloaked man, who takes great care as to not reveal his appearance, grows not weary, as I would not from such an easy task. But is this man not old? He spoke of attending a wedding ceremony during the time of Sigmund, before Sigurd was yet of this world. Although, other concerns press upon my mind. Fafnir will soon arrive.

    I would much like to rid this world of Sigurd and escape these woods long before Fafnir came to know of our trespass. Time for such an outcome is running out. I cannot attack now for the two men conceal the holes with heavy branches and dead and decaying undergrowth. The risk of attacking two men who may prove as equals is too high. Yet if

LEGEND OF FENRIR

Sigurd crawls into his hole, I would be at the disadvantage for his weapon will be at the ready awaiting Fafnir. I continue to watch the men as they conceal the last of the trenches. Sigurd slaps his horse on its flank and with a snort, it carries on down the path back from where they came, rounds the bend, and remains out of sight from where Fafnir approaches. The cloaked man steps up to Sigurd and lays a hand upon his shoulder.

"I have many great things planned for you, hero." He motions Sigurd into his hole. The slayer of my children slumps into the poisoned earth and the cloaked man conceals him. When finished, he takes his leave down the path leading south and out of the forest. A quick jolt shoots through my body for an opportunity presents itself to attack the cloaked man now while Sigurd is hidden away. He is close, but not close enough to catch completely unaware. If I pounced, he would have time to react, in whatever capacity he is able. Regardless, in this last moment before he will prove out of reach, the only thought consuming my mind is that he helped orchestrate the deaths of my sons. For that act he cannot leave alive. I turn myself towards him and, as he rounds the bend in the path back towards me, I ready myself on all fours, hands and feet in the dirt, ready to shift.

A terrible roar rents the air. Fafnir has come. I fall flat against the ground watching the man who looks over my head, taking no notice of me. He turns forward and continues on his way out of the forest without a lick of fear. Once out of range, I spin to face the path where Sigurd hides. The path upon which Fafnir treads. Another roar engulfs the air just a short way down the path. He will soon be upon us. I take one last moment to conceal myself behind a thick tree and amidst the bushes so that I cannot be seen, though, it will hamper my attack when the time comes.

In wake of the dragon's roars comes a subtle tremble

PETER CURSON

in the earth. The dragon's footfalls are enough to shake the ground. Large indeed he must be. It matters not. Once he is above the hole, Sigurd will attack and spill the dragon's guts. And when he attempts escape from his hole, I will descend upon Sigurd. Come Fafnir, and let us be done with it.

    From the ground, I cannot see the path. Oh, how I wish I could shift. My wolf ears would pick out the dragon's very breaths and I would know exactly how far he is. All I can hear now is the wind blowing from the east. Intuitively, I sniff and gag hard. What a putrid stink! Holding down my stomach, I risk another sniff. No, this is not wind. It is the dragon's breath. And now I hear him. Fafnir approaches from but thirty paces away. He nears so close that I can hear his nostrils flare with each heavy breath. I hear his feet shuffling in the dirt. This is it. The time has come. But I need to see him with my two eyes.

    I shuffle ever so slightly around the tree and see him there, right there on the path. He stands larger than me, with scales of the deepest red covering him like shield upon shield. His tail, as long as his body, slithers behind him with spikes running from its tip, up his spine, to his head. Horns protrude from his skull in all directions like a lion's mane. His jaw, hanging slightly open, reveals layers of teeth sharper than my canines and a dark purple, squirming tongue. His nostrils, large and round, widen with each breath, and at the base of his snout are his eyes, malicious, colored dark orange like the fire within his breast.

    My chest tightens and my body trembles. I clench my fists resisting the necessity to shift. In the presence of such a creature, how can I stay naked and vulnerable and so small? For the first time here on Midgard, I am scared. But I must remain small and hidden if this is to work. He does not know I am here. He suspects nothing. I am safe so long as I do not shift—a predicament I have never known.

LEGEND OF FENRIR

The ground shakes and intensifies with each nearing step. I fear that the traps will falter and Fafnir will spot the holes and trenches. Surely, it would not mean my doom if Sigurd is discovered prematurely. Fafnir would kill Sigurd with but a moment of intense fire. Yet as much as I would love to see the cretin roast in dragon fire, his head is mine. Fafnir has no claim on Sigurd's life. I do. Even if it means battling the dragon for him, I will be the one to kill Sigurd.

Fafnir steps between the trenches, then steps again. The covers remain intact. All is well. His broad legs pound the ground and his claws dig deep into the hardened soil. Within three more thunderous steps, he will stand directly over Sigurd and his weakness, his soft underbelly, will be exposed. In truth, I do not think his hide would prove soft. I surmise my claws would have trouble tearing apart Fafnir's flesh. But Gram, Sigurd's runic sword with all its power, will surely slice as easily as a scythe in a field of wheat.

As he nears Sigurd, the tree blocks my view of Fafnir. One step. Two. Quicker than I should, I shuffle to the other side of the tree. A twig snaps. Fafnir stops his leg midair and turns his head in my direction. My predatory instincts take over. I cannot control it. I burst forth from my hiding place and shift causing Fafnir's eyes to widen. Seeing the shock in the dragon's eyes fills me with an energy so fierce it propels my legs towards him without hesitation. Fafnir takes in a breath of air and in its throat smolders an intensifying orange glow. Fire. I push off the ground and pounce with claws spread wide and as I do, I hear a guttural shout and twigs burst from beneath Fafnir's foot. Sigurd rises from his hole, thrusting Gram glowing red straight into Fafnir's shoulder. The dragon recoils from the strike and with an unfathomable roar, he unleashes a stream of fire from his mouth, barely missing me due to his recoil. I land on the dragon's neck and the dragon falls backwards. I attempt attack on the dragon's throat

PETER CURSON

but for such a large monster, he is quick to roll, throwing me off him. I crash into a tree, causing it to topple.

Scampering to my feet, I witness Sigurd jumping out of his hole and rolling as Fafnir sends fire his way. With Gram in hand, he advances on the dragon and slashes at his flank. To great surprise, the dragon slides backwards in the dirt from the impact, but his scales protect him from grievous injury. The dragon's hind leg falls into one of the trenches and in this moment of vulnerability, I run and pounce again, landing atop his back. I do not attempt attack for I know it would be futile. Fafnir instinctively shakes to throw me off him once more, but I am ready. I lift myself off the beast as he reacts, bend my legs, and push off the dragon straight for Sigurd. He jumps out of the way and rushes towards Fafnir. He will not face me! Though, as I would, Sigurd moves to attack the greater of his two opponents.

He dives to the ground, breaking the covers over one of the trenches and attempts to strike Fafnir from underneath. I bring my eyes back to the dragon who already moves against me. He spins on his feet, swinging his hind towards me, his tail following as would a whip. I duck down, my belly against the dirt, and I dodge the first strike. Yet he raises his tail and slams it down upon my back, pinning me to the ground. With a roar, I attempt to raise myself but cannot lift off the ground. Fafnir takes notice of Sigurd and at once blows fire at the ground. Sigurd is forced to retreat out of the trenches and away from the dragon. In this moment of distraction, I roll onto my side and with me, Fafnir's tail turns, revealing its underside. Arching my neck, I open my jaws and sink my teeth deep into the beast's tail. He growls and sharply tugs his tail from my jaws, my teeth ripping his flesh apart as he does.

His blood drips from my mouth. At once, I fear that his very blood may be poison but it neither tastes putrid nor toxic. In fact, my pains subside and my vigor returns to me

LEGEND OF FENRIR

with such strength I have never before felt. Without another thought, I turn from the dragon and charge against Sigurd. He readies himself and as I maneuver to pounce from his flank, he moves against me. I slash with my paw, he with his sword, and we both hit the other. Only one of my claws strike, tearing apart his mail shirt, small rings flying in all directions. His sword slices my flank. But unlike the first time he successfully landed a strike against me when battling me and my sons, I feel very little pain. I attack at once, much to the surprise of Sigurd for his strike proved ineffective. He dodges to the side and as he does, I hear a haunting noise.

From Fafnir's mouth spews a mist of green and purple aimed at me. I pivot and attempt escape but some of the mist falls upon my back. How badly it stings! My legs give in from pain. I push from side to side, rolling in the dirt to rid my fur of the poison. The ground trembles beneath me so I recover to my feet. Fafnir has turned his tail and sprints back the way he came with incredible speed. I turn to find Sigurd in this chaos and he rushes past upon his horse, galloping faster than any horse I have seen, save Odin's horse Sleipnir. I howl and dash down the path, gaining speed as I go.

It does not take long to gain upon Sigurd. He checks over his shoulder every few seconds to how much closer I have come, how much time he has left until I catch him. I suspect he will make a move—abruptly halt his horse and attack me before I have time to react. But he does not make such a move, or any move. He simply moves against Fafnir. A lust for death consumes his eyes but that lust is not directed at me. Perhaps he reserves it solely for Fafnir. Yet as I near, his horse becomes aware of how close I truly am and kicks off ever faster, matching my own speed. We carry on as such, following Fafnir through the winding path with no question it leads to his hoard.

PETER CURSON

He remains only several seconds ahead of us. In a moment, Fafnir breaks through a tree line and into the middle of an expansive field within the forest, void of any green, growing thing much like the region surrounding this forest. Fafnir turns at once and awaits our arrival. Sigurd breaks through the tree line and stops his horse in its tracks. I enter the field and stop as well for behind Fafnir, I see it: his hoard. Never have I seen so much gold in one heap. The hoard is so considerable that even the wealth of all the Kings of the North could not match it. This is the dwarven gold that he protects. The gold that has cursed him. Fafnir raises his head and roars, spewing fire high into the air, painting the sky orange.

"*Varulv!*" Sigurd shouts. "We cannot defeat this beast alone. We have to fight as one if we are to survive."

"I care not for defeating this dragon! Your death is all I desire."

"And perhaps you would take it, but at the cost of your own life if Fafnir remains alive. Come, let us press attack!"

He does not wait for my response and rides straight for the dragon. A flurry of thoughts rush through my mind in less than a second. Should I leave Sigurd to battle Fafnir alone and let the dragon kill him? It will allow me to escape this wretched forest alive. But turning tail to the man who slayed my sons is something I cannot do. No. Fleeing will not avenge my sons. I must be the one to kill Sigurd. And the only way to kill him is to kill the dragon first.

ELEVEN

Flames leap up from the ground. The inferno consumes all. Trees burn. Stones tremble. Smoke rises high to the clouds, towering the largest of signal fires, but this day no one rides to our rescue. The battlefield, licked by flames, is clouded by waves of heat, screens of haze, and fires burning taller than me. The dragon keeps near his hoard and spews fire as his sole means of defense turning this place into a battlefield of coals. But through the fire and flames comes one advantage: a clouded field of vision. Sigurd takes advantage of his small size and together we circle around the beast with dragon fire at our backs in order to ignite Fafnir's lair in a blaze to the point where he stands amidst fire from all around with no sight of us.

   The sound of fire and cackling wood drown out my already silent steps. Sigurd distances himself from me and we near the beast. Such immense heat drains the energy from me and with each step, fear seeps through. How can I fight in the midst of such heat against a foe who appears impervious? A

PETER CURSON

loud roar answers my question. He sees me. I pounce to my left, away from Sigurd, and a stream of fire follows. Sigurd takes this chance to advance upon the dragon but even through all this noise I can hear the tattered remains of his mail shirt, and so does Fafnir. The stream of fire turns his way and my instincts propel me to attack. I dig into the scorched earth and push myself forward straight for the dragon and launch myself with claws spread. I strike but only manage to scratch his impenetrable scales.

As I land behind Fafnir, I notice in the corner of my eye Sigurd pressing attack. With a quick pivot, I move to attack as well but Fafnir is quick to maneuver and swings his tail in a wide arc. I am quick enough to dodge but Sigurd upon his two legs cannot. The tail smashes him hard, sending him to the edge of the field. This is my chance to finish it. With the dragon and his hoard behind me, I sprint for Sigurd who struggles to raise himself. The smoke stings my watering eyes and my vision falters. The red glow of his sword is all I can keep in focus. I roar loud and snap my jaw. Nothing. I squeeze the water from my eyes and see Sigurd scrambling to his feet and running for the dragon. He is only safe from my jaws when close to the dragon's. What a miserable fate.

A sliver of doubt enters my mind. A brief hesitation. Should I resign from this battle? If only Fafnir knew I seek Sigurd's life and not his. Then we need not attack each other. Though, in his curse-fed craze, I doubt he holds any comprehension behind that scaly skull. But my strength indeed drains quickly with each breath. Unnaturally so. I wobble and my visions whirls. Why do I falter when mere moments ago I was stronger than I have ever been? The dragon's blood. It gave me strength. It dulled my pain. And now it wears off and I feel the true weariness that afflicts my body. Another drop of blood, that is all I need and I can finish this fight. I have to. For Sköll and Hati.

LEGEND OF FENRIR

Sigurd turns his head and sees me gaining upon him fast, faster than he can near the dragon. If he turns and faces me, Fafnir will surely kill him. If he keeps on, I will. He shouts as loud as his puny body can and he waves his sword, catching the dragon's attention. Seeing us advance as such, the dragon thinks this an offensive against him and with a deep breath, he sends fire towards us. We dodge in different directions. I press attack now and hope with all my being that Sigurd does as well for how can the dragon defend from two sides? Through the fire and smoke, I see a faint glimmer from Gram. Sigurd indeed advances. But Fafnir chooses me as a target. Another stream of fire. I am forced to the side and away from my target but he cannot keep his focus solely on me. Before he averts his attention from me, his fire ceases and in its wake, his poisonous mist clouds the area in front of me. He turns his neck towards Sigurd thinking he has bought himself a few seconds before needing to fend me off once more. A grievous mistake.

Gaining my bearing, I close my eyes and rush through the mist. Pain meets me at once and all I can do to fight against my impulses to retreat from this toxic cloud is let out a terrible roar and push forward. However, the pain disorients me and I quickly lose myself, forcing me to open my eyes to find the dragon. The mist blinds me in seconds. But in those seconds, I see Fafnir and his neck is exposed. Three strides next, I feel his mound of gold beneath my paws and leap upon it and with a great thrust I jump straight for Fafnir. I reopen my eyes so blurred I can only see colors. A movement of red catches my attention and guided by my instincts, I swipe. I connect. Flesh rips apart between my claws followed by incredible heat. Landing hard against the ground, I scramble to my feet and retreat a distance but the heat has turned into a raging pain. I have caught fire.

Five agonizing strides next, I exit the fiery field and fall to my side, rolling back and forth until the scorching

PETER CURSON

ceases, leaving a tortuous burn in its wake. With the side of my paws, I wipe the tears and the sting from my eyes and as I do, I feel my paw is wet. Now able to open my eyes without enduring searing pain, I see it drenched in blood. Dragon blood. Looking back to Fafnir, he swings his tail wildly to keep Sigurd at bay, all the while attempting to breath fire and poison without success. I left a deep wound in his neck, blood flowing freely. With each exhale, small amounts of poison mist escape the wound, as well as flames. His breath is rendered useless.

Fafnir lands another hit on Sigurd and turns his attention to me. He sees me kneeling and in unfathomable pain. The wound I dealt and the pain he feels throws him into an uncontrollable rage. He surges straight for me. The ground shakes, causing me to fall. But in this moment, my nostrils flare at the scent of Fafnir's blood upon my paw. I do not hesitate in licking it. Mere seconds is all it takes. I am up on my feet. No more weariness holds me down. No more pain keeps me back. The dragon roars. I howl. And we charge against one another.

Despite this spike in energy, I know in my bones I cannot defeat the dragon in a test of strength. I move to maneuver around the beast and Sigurd catches my eye scrambling behind the hoard of gold and I know his plan at once—the same plan he had all along. So I maneuver around the dragon but instead of pressing attack, I carry on behind Fafnir and sprint right for his gold. An outcry of hate and disbelief erupts from the dragon and the ground quakes harder than before as he chases me faster than I could have ever imagined a dragon could go. Fear grips me that he might catch me first. His jaw snaps behind me. Tucking my tail between my legs, I push onwards and reach the mound of gold. In two strides, I crest the mound and leap forward. Fafnir follows, clamoring up the hoard. As he reaches the top, the coins and treasures tumble

LEGEND OF FENRIR

like a rockslide and the dragon's feet falter, casting him forward where Sigurd lay in wait gripping Gram tight. The dragon falls over the warrior, his belly now exposed. Sigurd rises and plunges Gram deep into the dragon's belly, carving him from chest to tail as the dragon's momentum carries him forward.

With one final quake, the dragon's carcass hits the ground dead and moves never again, his blood draining from his body into the blackened soil. His scales darken and his hide withers and the fire in his eyes diminishes leaving nothing but black abyss in its wake. He is gone, and with him, the curse. But victory has not yet been achieved. Not for me.

The clang of metal brings my attention from the dragon. Sigurd attempts escape. But with the power of the dragon's blood still fresh upon my lips, I will not allow it. I sprint after him, chasing him back into the forest. He whistles loud and there to meet him is his horse. Sigurd mounts it and they take off down the path. Whereas before I could not maintain pace with the horse, now I find myself faster. I close the gap and a smile grows upon my face. He is mine.

Now so close to the horse, its stench fills my nose. It sparks something in my mind. It is somehow so familiar. It recalls old memories. Memories from my time in Asgard? No. Memories from when I first journeyed to Hélheim.

I remember.

As the realization hits me, the horse kicks off the ground and gallops into the air! This is the offspring of Sleipnir himself. But lineage does not grant this horse escape this day. I take a great stride, plant my paws in the soil and with the last of the dragon's strength in my muscles, I leap off the ground and sink my claws into the horse's hind, bringing us both to the ground. Sigurd tumbles into the middle of the path, his sword far from reach. He attempts to rise but his body fails him, causing him to collapse. Casting the wounded horse aside, I rush to the human and plant my paw hard on his chest, pinning him to the forest floor. He pounds my paw with his fists but soon resigns his fight, the last of his energy escaping him. He lays his head backwards in the dirt struggling to breathe.

"Is that all?" I ask. "Is there no more fight in you, human? Will you not fight until your last breath as my sons did? Will you not fight until lacerated and bloodied?"

"I have fought," he replied "It was I who slayed the dragon. Not you. You are simply picking up my scraps like a wild dog. I was not so when I slayed your sons! I fought against both of them at once and arose the victor even after you came to their aid. They deserved to die, your sons. They attacked innocent people. They tormented them. Your sons had to be stopped."

"I was innocent too, upon a day, having done no wrong thing in my life. And look what has become of me! All I have ever loved has been taken from me. All I have gained in this life, snatched from my grip. Taken. All taken. And the two most important things to me in this life were taken by your hand." I sink my claws into his flesh and drag him through the dirt towards his sword. He screams in terrible pain and reaches for his sword in a pathetic attempt at saving himself. With my other paw, I stomp on his arm and hear the snapping of his bones. "I could claw you in pieces. I could rip you apart. I could devour you limb by limb or swallow you whole. But that will not do my sons justice." His eyes widen in horror as my form shifts back to my two-legged self—this being the first time he has seen me in my normal form. I stoop down and pick up his sword. Sheer power surges into my body as Gram's red glow bursts forth, intensifying as my malice consumes me. I lay the tip of his sword upon his neck.

"Who are you?" he asks, the fight within him now all but spent.

"I am Fenrir. Convey this name to Odin along with

LEGEND OF FENRIR

the warning of my jaws." I bring the sword back and thrust. A force knocks me over. Another person. I am quick to cast him off me and regain my stance. Standing between Sigurd and me stands not a man, but a woman wearing a mail shirt wielding a broad sword and a round shield upon which is painted a wolf. From her helmet flows long crimson hair and in her fierce brown eyes I see captured within them the spirit of the forest and the essence of all things that grow. And I recognize her instantly.

"Kára?"

Her eyes widen with disbelief. She can barely bring herself to say my name, but finally her guard lowers and a whisper escapes her lips. "Fenrir? Is this really you standing before me?"

I drop the sword in my hand and approach her. I take off her helmet and surely there is her face which my mind could not fully remember. It is not as delicate as it once was, nor as soft. Before me she stands hardened as if tempered within a forge. She stands a shieldmaiden.

I drop to my knees and take her hand. "I am sorry, Kára, for all that has befallen you. It is all my fault. I am to blame. It was Thor's hatred for me that caused him to strike you down. He did it to hurt me. I am cursed. All who draw near to me are thrown to turmoil and misery. What I would do to give you back your wings and to see you returned to Asgard. I am so truly, deeply sorry."

She places her hand upon my head and runs it gently through my hair. "It seems you have not had your hair properly washed since last we were together." I wince at the memory of how I left her. She moves her hand to my chin and guides me to my feet. "You are not cursed, Fenrir. Thor, and Thor alone, is to blame for what happened to me. It saddens my heart that guilt has plagued your heart all these days."

"Perhaps upon a day. But no longer. Guilt is now but

PETER CURSON

a fleeting shadow with naught but hatred and vengeance to fill its place, consuming my very being. I seek only one thing: vengeance. And that is something you currently impede."

She steps back away from me. "For what reason do you move against Sigurd?" Her tone has changed and it leaves me uneasy.

"For what reason do you defend him?"

"Sigurd, he is my betrothed; I have pledged myself to him. On that day when I lost my wings and became human, I was caught in the chaos of battle. I ran away to a nearby town, but the army at my back was soon defeated and their enemy raided the town. The elderly were slain, the kids taken captive for slaves. And the women… Two men chased me through the street and they caught me. But in an instant, I saw them fall to the ground and Sigurd stood there with a troop of his men fighting the raiders back. He saved my life, Fenrir. I told him everything about me and he took me with him in order to protect me and to teach me how to live in this world. He taught me how to fight, how to defend myself so no man could ever lay his hands upon me again. And I have fought beside him in all his battles ever since—until recently when he left to hunt monsters in the North, not allowing me to accompany him. He barely came back with his life. And then he left again to slay the dragon. I could not bear the thought of losing him, so I came after him. When I saw the tower of smoke rising from this place, I feared the worst. I ran here as fast as my legs could carry me and when I finally find Sigurd, I see you standing over him with sword at the ready. So I ask you again, why do you move to kill him?"

The words catch on my tongue. I have not had to utter them before aloud so I say them as straight as I can. "He killed my sons." She looks at me surprised. Surprised about the fact that I had sons or that Sigurd killed them, I cannot tell. "The monsters he was sent to slay, they were Sköll and Hati, my

LEGEND OF FENRIR

sons. It was by his blade they died and now it will be by his blade they are avenged. Step aside, Kára." I brush past her and approach Sigurd. He attempts to sit up but his broken ribs and arm prevent him from doing so. With a stomp, I set my leg upon his chest once more. He does not take his eyes from mine. In them I see a resolve that matches even that of Týr himself. For all the atrocities this human has committed against me, he truly is a warrior among warriors.

Kára walks up to me, though she does not raise her weapon. "I know I cannot stop you through force. Thor had trouble with that on his own. But listen to me Fenrir, do not let hate consume you, as you say. Hate is a beast with a hunger that cannot be satisfied. The more you feed it, the hungrier it becomes. Surely if you search your heart you can find truth in that. Let this be the first step you take to control your own life. You are not cursed. You can make your own destiny."

My eyes lower to the ground for a moment. Destiny. Fate. That which I have wrestled with since that dreaded day my siblings and I were captured by the Gods of Asgard. Is there a point anymore, to wrestle with such unknown forces? Does life not move forward regardless of who pulls the strings? All I know is that Sigurd's life rests in my hands. It is my hand that will grant him the mercy of life or kill him where he lies. I will not have Sigurd believe that Fate has saved him or doomed him. It is me, Fenrir the Jötunn.

Lifting my head, I bring my gaze to meet Kára's. Her eyes look deep into mine in silent persuasion. Now I surprise myself for a slight chuckle escapes my lips. "If there was ever a person in all the Nine Worlds whose words could reach my heart, it would be yours."

A small smile creeps upon her face. Until she sees my eyes harden.

"But I swore an oath to my sons."

She shouts but her words do not reach my ears. I turn

PETER CURSON

to Sigurd and without hesitation I plunge his sword through his neck. Blood gurgles in his throat, spilling out of the wound and down his neck, staining the ground below. His body twitches for several moments until his pain-ridden eyes cease to blink and the blood escaping his neck flows no longer, leaving his face pale and mouth hanging wide as through still trying to breathe.

    It does not help. The searing pain in my heart remains as strongly as it did before. My sons are still gone and they are not yet avenged. Sigurd, my sons' killer, lies dead beneath me, but he did not orchestrate their deaths. It was the cloaked man. The one who re-forged his father's sword with the runes. Only one being in the Nine Worlds understand the runes. The man was none other than Odin in disguise. He gave Sigurd the offspring of his own horse Sleipnir. He gave Sigurd a weapon capable of bringing down any foe. He sent Sigurd to slay my sons. And now the path before me clears. There is only one thing left to do. One life yet to take: the chief of the gods. Odin.

TWELVE

Sköll was quite the son. He wanted to be the first to do anything. He always awoke first, the first to eat and the first to finish, and he was the first out of the house to go hunting. He was even the first to speak. But not Hati. Hati was patient. He took the time to appreciate and savor all things in life, from the food he ate to the hunts he led in the wild.

I saw myself in both of them, as well as Hyrrokkin. They inherited her strength and resolve. We were quite the family. Conflict arose from time-to-time, as they do in all families, even more so with a family of predators. But I have never seen more loyal sons than Sköll and Hati. Despite their young age and not understanding all that had happened to me and their mother, nor the complexities of the situation they were born into, they never once waivered in their love and loyalty to Hyrrokkin and me.

In this moment of victory and exhaustion, my mind is finally able to escape the plague of misfortune surrounding me, and it cannot help but wander. Memories both good and

PETER CURSON

bad fill my mind from the birth of my sons to the day I saw them banished. I wonder how life would have been today if Thor and his sons had not attacked us that night, setting off the events that led to Sköll and Hati's trial. Would we still live as we had been, under Odin's rule and watching life pass by? Would the Jötnar have marched against Asgard? Would Sköll and Hati still be alive?

Perhaps. But whether it was that day or the next, Thor would have found another way to banish my sons. If not for humiliating his sons in a wrestling match, the reason would have been by playing on the fear of the Æsir. The Æsir feared for their lives having three giant Jötunn wolves in their midst, yet we were the ones who were not safe. From the day they were born to the day they were slain, my sons were not safe and the only comfort I now have is that all the Æsir, including Odin and Thor, now share that fear for I have escaped. And there is no doubt in their mind I will return to claim my vengeance. Alongside the armies of Jötunheim and Hélheim, we will destroy them and my hate will be satisfied.

Kára has knelt over her betrothed for the past several minutes. I do not hear a sob nor see a tear, yet I can sense the turmoil within her breast. I took someone she loved, maybe the only person in this world she loved. Just as Sigurd did to me. I do not, however, sense hatred coming from Kára, nor do I sense it building within her. She kneels now as I knelt over my sons as they passed. Will she swear to avenge Sigurd? Will she now press attack against me? She knows the latter would be a futile attempt; she has already said she cannot stop me through force. It seems that is the reason I stay here: to see what Kára has to say. I have spent the past years wondering about her and wishing I could apologize for her misfortune and rectify it if I could. And now, this. There is nothing I can do for her now. I am to her as Sigurd was to me. Yet what will

LEGEND OF FENRIR

she do once she tears herself from Sigurd's corpse? With no intention of fighting me, I expect she will simply move on and leave without a word. What would I do if I was her, powerless to enact revenge? Get help. Seek the enemy of my enemy. Will she attempt to return to Asgard as I will return to Jötunheim? Perhaps she will join the ranks of the Einherjar herself so she may one day fight against me and my people. Regardless of her future intentions, I can only see mourning as part of her present intentions. So then truly, why do I stay? Why am I not on my way to find a shaman to send me back to Hélheim now that I have concluded my business with Sigurd?

Kára. She is the only thing in this world that I hold a connection to. She is someone who I once cared about. One of my only friends. She saw me as Fenrir in a world who only saw me as a monster. That is why I stay. I am alone. Until I return to my wife's arms, I am alone. And when I do, will she ever forgive me for failing in saving her sons?

Indeed, until I return to Hyrrokkin and she forgives me, I am alone.

At last, I raise myself from the ground, catching Kára's attention. I shift. And with a wobbly step, I start to make my way down the path but hesitate. "I will avenge you, Kára. My road leads me to Asgard and the very gates of Innangard. When the world of the Æsir stands about me in flames, I will seek out Thor and he will pay with his life for what he has done to you. Yet, the deaths of all the Æsir will not account for the loss of your wings, nor will their deaths account for the loss of my sons. Though, it is all I can do in this life. Perhaps you will be proven right, that my hatred will never be satisfied. But I will not stop. I cannot stop. And when Asgard lies in ruins and all the Æsir are dead at my feet, if my vengeance is still not quenched, then I will find contentment knowing I did all in my power to right the wrongs of my enemies and of my own. Farewell, dearest Valkyrie. May you one day find peace.

PETER CURSON

I fear I never will."
  With head and tail low, I start the next leg of my journey leaving Kára behind. For your sake, Kára, may we never meet again.

  Where on Midgard am I? I know I am in the northern regions of Svealand as Hél mentioned, but am I east as Birca is, or am I west like Hälsingborg? Regardless, I set off south across the poisoned plains that mar the land between Fafnir's forest and the rest of Svealand's forests, leaving the cursed gold behind. I wonder what will become of it without a guardian. Perhaps an unsuspecting human will chance upon it, becoming ensnared in the curse himself. Would it form him also into a dragon, or another fearsome creature? Musings without answers, but they do keep my mind occupied until I find myself in this land. Once I find a town, I will learn of where I am, then I can make my way back to find the shaman. Or perhaps I will find another one who can send me back to Hélheim. It will not take much persuasion.

  The evergreens of Svealand are a welcome smell. Fafnir's forest was void of life, taken by the curse on that dwarfish gold, and thus had no pleasant smells. Now the scent of pine meets my nostrils and I cannot help but stop and inhale deeply. The soil beneath my paws is soft and cool to the touch. I cannot explain it, but now that I have left Fafnir's cursed lands, I can feel life within the soil. The nutrients, the insects, the moisture. I smell life within the foliage. I taste life in the air. It reminds me of my own forest back in Asgard. So alive and luscious. One day I would like to return there after the war. It must be teeming with reindeers! I was the only predator in those woods. I can almost taste them now upon my tongue, which makes me all the more hungry. Time to find some food.

  One bear later, my stomach is not yet full but very

LEGEND OF FENRIR

glad. Fighting a dragon takes a toll, even for a giant wolf, and unfortunately, the bears have only just started fattening themselves for the winter ahead. Soon they will be fat and juicy and I will have my fill.

The sky turns darker, which does not mean much in these summer days, yet it acts as a signal for my body, causing me to feel the full weight of my weariness. Dragon blood sure is a miraculous thing and not only gave me unimaginable power in the moment of battle, but it surely carried me until now on an empty stomach. It seems it indeed is time for me to plop down and rest. No one is around, not this close to the dragon's lands, so I find the comfiest patch of dirt and close my eyes. I fall asleep instantly.

I do not know if it was because of my exhaustion until now or that my mind was finally at rest after killing Sigurd, but last night's sleep was the best I have had since my days in Asgard. It was rest in the truest sense of the word. Worries of my sons' safety nor thoughts of revenge engaged my mind. Everything ceased. And now as it is well past dawn, I am refreshed and can tackle the days to come.

The journey southward this day is surprisingly pleasant. With proper rest and meal and the wide forest to venture through, my mind settles. It is a peace I have not known for quite some time, perhaps since my days in Asgard. Indeed, I am not at peace nor will I be for a time yet. But this peace of mind comes from the absence of unanswerable questions. From the day I set foot on Midgard, questions swirled in my mind. Where are my sons? Should I have gone east and not west? What if I left Asgard when they were born? What if I never took a wife. What if I fought Odin to the death instead of resigning and followed Hél to her domain?

But no longer. All questions revolving around my

PETER CURSON

sons and their deaths have been answered. And to those unanswerable "what ifs," I have made my peace knowing I will never find those answers, for they hold no answers. Whether it was through my choices or by Fate's will or by both at once, the past remains as such and cannot be changed. So why dwell upon it? I will not look backwards while life moves forward. While I move forward. And right now, forward means south. Forward means towards a shaman. Forward means towards Hél and eventually Jötunheim where my wife remains waiting.

Ah, Jötunheim. It remains but a name to me. From a far I have seen it while upon Odin's throne but how limiting a fleeting glimpse is in my memory. What good is seeing a forest without feeling the soil beneath me or hearing the rustling of the leaves in the breeze. And what about the mountain peaks covered in frost and snow or even the barren plains teeming with creatures and the skies full of vultures. Seeing from a safe distance is an easily forgotten thing. But when I am there in the midst of a wild world where even I may fall prey to the beasts of the land, that is what my memory will remember. That is where I feel alive. That is where I belong.

Midgard is a beautiful place full of many wonders and sights and smells and noises. Just like any of the Nine Worlds, Midgard has creatures and landscapes and food that is unique to this world and this world alone. And would there be but time to explore Midgard, I would, for surely there is more to this world than the North where the forests are evergreen and the mountains are rugged and cold. However, I feel my time here is near its end. No time will I waste in returning to my wife and then to war with the vast army of my kin by my side. Though, when the war is won and all I have set out to accomplish is finished, I know I will return with Hyrrokkin to explore what else Midgard has to show in the days long after my wrath is satisfied.

Things never will be the same again no matter how

LEGEND OF FENRIR

much I long for it. Sköll and Hati will never again be by my side. Kára will never again flutter her wings. My family will never again be together. I wonder how Angrboda fares. I had not heard word of her during my time in Asgard. She could have stayed in her hall in Asgard's countryside, but why would she? We remained there in Asgard for Loki's sake. But with her children gone and Loki still choosing to remain close to the gods, why would she stay? I hope she left. I hope she returned to Jötunheim, her homeland that she loved so much. She deserves that happiness. And I cannot wait to find her there.

After days of constant journeying through forest and over field, I find myself on the shore of the sea. It seems I have ventured eastward during my walk, now appearing somewhere on Svealand's eastern shore. It does not prove familiar to my eyes or nose, so I must stand somewhere north of Birca.

Resting here on the rocky shore with the smell of salt upon the refreshing breeze brings Jor to the front of my mind. It was not that long ago that I last saw him, after his battle with Thor. Perhaps I should venture to the south of Gautland once more to seek him out. I would greatly like him to join me in my return to Jötunheim. But he may not hold it to the same height as I do. His last words to me ring in my ears: "The sea is the only home I have left, and I will not leave it." But if I know one thing about my brother, it is that he is as stubborn as a rock, and probably dumber. Surely he would follow me knowing that I return to Jötunheim to wage war against the Æsir. Even if not as a brother, he would follow me as any Jötunn would. For what reason would he remain here in Midgard to suffer his exile? Yes. I will make my way south once more.

It appears that means I will follow my own footsteps. I shall return to Birca, procure another boat and sail down to

PETER CURSON

Gautland once more, taking more care not to lose my boat to the Gautar again. A handful of days it will cost me, but for the chance to reunite with my brother and begin rebuilding my family, it is well worth the time. And I find myself smiling. With Jor alongside me when we find a shaman and force him to send us to Hél, the three of us will be together again. For the first time since that horrid day, we will be together. I long for that reunion. And it may soon be upon us.

No sooner after I take my first step to depart the shoreline do I hear a strange sound from high above me. I look to the sky and see the white clouds darkening. My instincts flare and bursting forth from the clouds comes a chariot led by two large goats with lightning sparking from the wheels. Thor's chariot. The Slayer of the Jötnar himself guides it down towards the ground with the reins in one hand and Mjölnir in the other. Behind him on either side stand his two sons. Magni holds a formidable chain over his shoulder and Modi, who has hated me more than his brother, holds an even larger chain at the ready. They have found me. I spin and sprint for the tree line while from atop the trees gallops a horse with eight legs carrying Odin as its rider. In his hand he holds Gungnir, his impeccable spear but it proves different than last I saw it. Now, it bears an ethereal gold glow about it as Sigurd's sword glowed red. And I see upon the tip of his spear runes glowing gold. I look to Odin and notice his eye widen at the sight of me, seeing how large and treacherous I have become since I last escaped his tyranny.

Instinctively, I pivot and launch myself to the left narrowly avoiding Sleipnir's hooves. I only manage three strides towards the forest before two trees topple and in their wake sprint Vidar and Vali, rushing straight for me. I manage to maneuver and change direction before they reach me. With Vidar and Vali to my left, Odin on my right, and Thor and his sons rushing behind me, I sprint straight for the cover of the trees

LEGEND OF FENRIR

where one last god presents himself.

Týr.

Dressed in battle clothes, he plants himself at the trees edge and awaits me. I have nowhere else to maneuver and I cannot stop running lest I am caught. With all the power in my legs, I push forward. Týr opens his arms wide ready to take me on and a moment next, we collide. To both of our surprises, I prove stronger and knock him far aside. Once upon a time not so long ago when faced with the same attack, he lifted me straight off the ground. I have grown strong indeed. But I am not yet strong enough to take on seven of the High-Æsir, which includes Odin himself. Without another thought, I carry on through the forest fleeing the gods.

Even though Vidar, Vali, and Týr are on foot, they keep pace with me. Their two legs prove slower than my four, but the forest is too congested for me to make quick escape, forcing me to knock down a host of trees while the gods easily traverse the forest between the trees. Above me, I hear Thor's chariot and the rattling of the chains. I will not lose them this way. Against all my instincts, I shift to my normal self, nearly tripping on my two feet from the speed, and carry on through the forest.

Much to my surprise, this results as an advantage. Even on two feet I am the faster runner and can now maneuver between the trees with ease. And though Thor and Odin can canvas the forest overhead faster than I can run, they will no longer see me under the forest canopy.

My senses are dull and limited and can no longer hear my pursuers above my own footfalls. With a couple glances over my shoulders, I see that Vidar and Vali press off in opposite directions attempting to flank me while Týr presses against me from behind. With this pace, I can outrun them. Anything that happens after I will tackle when the time comes. For now, all I must do is run. Another look over my shoulder

PETER CURSON

and I have lost Vidar and Vali, and Týr is almost lost to me as well. I hear two deafening calls and as I turn forward, two black blurs collide with my face, clouding my vision with black feathers. Huginn and Muninn. They try to rip at my flesh with their talons, slapping me with their wings as they drift in front of me. I cover my face with one arm and reach out and grab one of them with the other. But before I can hurl him to the ground and beneath my foot, the brother pecks at my arm, tearing off flesh. I quickly grab the both of them and cast them both into a thick bush full of thorns, hearing their screeches of pain as I sprint away. And no sooner than three strides next, I hear rushing footsteps and a large body collides with me. As I fall, I feel fur and hear a snarl. And I smell the unmistakable smell of one of Odin's wolves. Whether it is Geri or Freki, I do not know. I toss it off me and as I raise myself, the second wolf tackles me once more, nearly missing my head with his jaws. I roll forward, forcing the wolf off me, and I shift. There is no helping it.

Keeping my momentum, I find my footing and sprint forward, smashing into Geri and Freki as I go. Now with my hearing back at its peak, I hear the two wolves following close behind and the ravens quickly catching up. And above, not far away, I hear the screaming goats guiding Thor's chariot right for me. This is not going to work. I cannot escape them like this. I have to fight back.

Ahead of me is a rather large clearing in the forest. The logical thing would be to avoid it and move further into the forest, and I hear Geri moving off in that direction while Freki presses behind me, hoping to drive me towards his brother. Yet I do not take the bait. I dash straight for the clearing. The goats yell again as they are forced in a new direction towards the clearing and they pick up tremendous speed. Thor hopes to beat me there. And I will allow him to do just that.

LEGEND OF FENRIR

Just as I near the clearing, the chariot flies above the trees, casting down its shadow upon me. When it overtakes me, I stride, plant my feet, and launch myself into the air, bursting up from the trees. Thor looks over his shoulder from the sudden noise but his sons are already facing me. Magni casts the chain around me as I fly towards the chariot. It wraps around my body as my paws hit the sides of the chariot, causing it to flip backwards and we all hurdle to the clearing below.

The impact sends pain vibrating through my body, but I have no time to waste. While Thor and his sons struggle beneath the chariot, I press against them. But I trip. My legs are caught in the chain! Knowing Odin is only seconds away riding upon his horse, I force my legs apart and with a snap, the chain breaks. I rise to my feet but Sleipnir descends upon me and this time, his hooves do not miss. They hit my head hard, nearly knocking me to the ground. But I cannot stop. I dash forward, crushing the chariot beneath me as I go, hearing the shouts of Thor and his sons below. I use the chariot as a stepping stone and launch myself towards the flying horse. With its eight legs, it is quick to maneuver out of reach of my jaws, but I swipe and hit the horse hard enough to cause Odin to fall off. When he lands, he loses grip of his spear and it hurdles into the forest.

Seeing him there, the man who caused my sons' deaths face down in the dirt sends me into a rage and I sprint for him. I fall upon him as he turns onto his back. He catches my paw with his two hands and holds me up, even as I force all my weight down upon him. But his arms tremble. He grows weak. I snarl loud and bar my teeth, saliva dripping from them onto Odin's face. He stares into my eyes with unrelenting strength and I find not a lick of fear in him. Though, as he struggles against me, he finds that I am indeed strong and no longer the same wolf he fought many moons ago. With a sharp movement, I push off of Odin's hands and slam down once more, sending his hands to his chest. I swoop my head down to his face but he raises me just enough to keep out of reach of my jaws. I can smell his sweat. I smell the stink of his horse. And soon I shall taste his head as it passes from mouth to stomach.

I slam down upon him once more causing his arms to falter and I bite down for the kill when I feel a sharp tug around my neck. I am forced backwards off of Odin and see upside down Modi holding the larger chain in his hands. I scramble up to rid myself of the chain but I feel one of its other ends cast upon my back. Magni. I twist and yet another part of this chain is cast about my hind with Vidar pulling tight, and seconds later Vali casts his end about my shoulders. The four of them spread out in opposite corners and pull hard upon the chain. My body, as big as it is, feels as though it will implode, my bones creaking and my muscles deforming between each iron link.

The thought to shift to my normal form enters my mind for surely when I shrink, I will have a moment of freedom. Though, the gods would collapse upon me and subdue me—if the chain does not crush me first. Nay, as a wolf I must break free.

I push off forward but they hold me in place. I scramble left and right. The Æsir slide in the dirt and shout in their struggle to hold me still. Yet they avail. I cannot break myself free of them!

"Cease!" a voice calls.

I look forward and see Odin standing there with Thor by his side holding Mjölnir with a gleeful smile upon his face I thought him incapable of forming.

"You and your sons have terrorized these lands for far too long," Odin says.

"Do not speak of my sons! It was you! You killed them. You gave Sigurd the blade that struck them down. You

LEGEND OF FENRIR

were behind it all from the day you banished my sons to this world. Was that your plan all along? Banish them to Midgard so you could find some willing human to slay them for you? And perhaps then you hatched the plan for Thor and his sons to waylay my sons and me in the streets as a pretext to banish them. You call me evil. You call me chaotic. *Utangard* as you say. Yet none in all the Nine Worlds stands more *utangard* than you, Odin. You are evil."

Movement from the trees catch my eye. It is Týr. He walks through the glade next to Odin and Thor but makes no sound and says nothing. I look into his eyes, which are locked upon my own. My only friend in Asgard and he takes part in the hunting party. Yet, I would expect no less from him. He would not sit idly by while his comrades hunt me, whether I be friend or foe. If he remains anything as he did years ago, he is here to ensure no one kills me on sight. Odin wants a trial and Týr will ensure that happens. It is surprising though that Odin would allow him, the man who aided in my escape, to take part in my capture.

"Fenrisulfr, it is time we take you back to Asgard to answer for your crimes against my Law."

I glance back to Týr. However, it seems his resolve remains strong and his mind set to purpose. I do not blame him—there is no other option for him but to align with his people and his leader. He looks at me with sympathy, as a friend would. But in this situation, he is not my friend. He is the God of War and Justice and will treat me as befits his title until my trial, which without any doubt ends in my death.

"Thor. Take him."

Thor jumps high into the air, far above any tree and as he falls, Mjölnir flashes with radiant blue light. I watch him descend and do not move until I see clearly the rage in his eyes. I push backwards at the last moment, dodging Thor. He shakes the ground with his fall, which causes his sons and half-brothers to lose their footing.

  This is my only chance. I throw myself to the left causing Vidar and Vali to fall on their faces, then right causing the same to Modi and Magni, and I take off towards the forest with the chain still hanging off me. I only make it five strides. The chain tugs hard against my body causing my front paws to lift off the ground. For only a moment, I look backwards and see Týr has taken the chain in two hands. My front paws land on the ground once more and I push forward, dragging an unrelenting Týr behind me. But then Vidar grabs the chain, and Vali as well, slowing my progress but they cannot stop me. They will not. Even as Thor and his sons take hold of the chain's loose ends, I drag the six of them in the dirt towards the forest where I can make my escape. Then Odin takes up the chain and holds me back. I cannot move.

  "Fen, your fight is over!" Týr shouts.

  He is wrong. My fight will never end, not until the last drop of blood escapes my veins and my heart ceases within my chest. I thrust forward, bearing the terrible pain with a guttural shout, and the chain snaps behind me. I tumble forward but recover in seconds, dashing into the cover of the trees. I rid myself of the iron strands left around me and put as much distance between myself and the Æsir as I can. But I will not be out of their grasp for long, and I know I will not achieve escape while Odin's pets chase me like this as a wolf, and worse yet in my normal form. My only chance is to hide from them, allow them to pass by, and escape in another direction.

  I run for several more moments until my nose picks up the smell of bear. I follow my nose straight to the bear's den and I shift to my two-legged self. The bear launches itself out of the den and charges at me. With a quick step to the side, I avert the bear's attack and I quickly pounce on its back, taking hold of its neck. I roll off its back and pull down, forcing the bear down to the ground belly-up. With one arm around

LEGEND OF FENRIR

its neck, I take my free hand and grasp its lower jaw and twist, breaking it.

The caws of the ravens advance at an alarming rate. With no time to kill the bear, I strike it hard on the muzzle, take hold of its fur with both hands, and haul it back to its den. The bear struggles and roars in pain. Now at the den, I crawl backwards into it, dragging the bear on top of me. The bear should hide me and mask my scent but the noise will give me away. With a series of harsh movements, I manage to spin the bear so that its belly lies atop my own. It attempts to swipe me with its paw but it has no room to move in here. I take hold of the bear's hanging, broken jaw, opening its mouth and shove my other hand straight down the bear's throat. It gags on my arm and cannot form any sort of noise. Just in time. I hear the flapping of wings pass by the den and shortly after the patter of paws. Some moments later, I hear the gods pass by along with the nickering of a horse and the stench of goat.

For a few more minutes I lie like this, my arm down the throat of a bear, just to be sure I have not been found. However, I cannot tarry long. Soon the wolves will lose my scent and the ravens will backtrack. I must be far from here when they do. But as I wait, my rage creeps upon me. The shock of attack and the scare of my near capture subside leaving anger in its wake. Odin wishes to put me to trial again! Does he not understand? All that has befallen his people and his world is from his own doing! If he had not banished my sons, I would not have escaped Innangard. If he had not sent Sigurd to slay my sons, I would have found them and left the humans far behind. But no longer. If my sons were taken from this world by the hands of Odin and the humans, I will reciprocate.

I retract my slimy arm from the bear's mouth and push it back out of the cave. With a quick movement, I end

PETER CURSON

the poor bear's misery and return it to its den as though nothing in this area had changed. There can be no clues left behind beyond those which I already have left.

West is the only direction for me to go. The sea lies to the east, endless forest to the north, and my enemies speed off south. All is well; the village where I found the shaman lies westward. Jormungand, it seems I will have to find you some time in the future when I have escaped the gods and they have long since passed this place in search of me. It is my sincerest hope the gods to not show up at your shore to find me. I do not think you would be smart enough to flee them to the depths of the ocean. Live, brother, and await my return. One day the three of us will be reunited.

But for now, the humans await their doom.

THIRTEEN

Rage is a dangerous thing. Not only does it feed on anything it can latch its claws on, it feeds upon itself, growing larger and larger still until it can no longer contain itself. It bursts forth from the vessel in which it broods and unleashes its fury by taking control of that very vessel. It will burn like a summer's fire upon the forest and will consume what lies before it until there is naught left to consume. Only then can it be quelled. Contained. But soon it will hunger once more.

My rage is no different. For the past two days, it has grown with each step. And I allowed it to do so. Do I not have reason to stoke the fire fueling my hatred? Do I not have just cause? There are times where rage and hatred should be avoided, situations where they will endanger you and set you to ruin. This is not one of those times. I am soon leaving this world but not without first sending as many humans to Hélheim as I can. My hatred for the humans and the gods they worship will push me into battle and my rage will see me rise victorious with blood flowing freely from my fangs. Though, I must enact my vengeance upon the humans with intelligence. Destroying village after village will only serve as a trail for the gods to find, one that leads straight to me. Nay, this is not the time for massacre and carnage—that will come with the war against the Æsir. Now is the time for a terror the humans will speak of for decades to come in hushed whispers, one that strikes from the darkness. One that kills mercilessly. One that they are powerless to stop.

On this second night since the gods attacked me, I arrive at the first village along my route. I must force myself to shift to my normal form in order to subdue my lust for bloodshed. The gods surely hunt me still and it will do me no good to mindlessly rampage through this village in the darkness for if even one human escapes, I will be undone. If Huginn and Muninn hear but one shrill cry of fright upon the wind, they will find me. I must first think this through and not simply sack and destroy as I did Hämnd. I wonder if anyone has stumbled upon the empty and desolate town yet.

And my plan materializes with that thought. How satisfying it is knowing that I annihilated an entire village, removing the people from this world in a single night. I left that place the only one knowing what happened there. If anyone has indeed ventured to Hämnd, the horror of what happened there will haunt them, following them wherever they go. Surely with the destruction I caused, they would attribute it to a monster, perhaps the *Varulv* himself. But what if they were to stumble on a village seemingly untouched except for the dead humans lying in their homes? That would be utter horror. No struggle. No fight. Only a silent death in the night. And after the flurry of questions settle, only one will remain: is our village next?

I enter the closest home. The door is loose and allows for a silent entry. The small home is just that. A fire nearly

LEGEND OF FENRIR

dead crackles in the center of the house with a pot of water over top. Furs and sheepskins cover the ground and a bench. A weaving loom poorly made stands near the far end of the house. Beyond it lies a wooden bed upon which sleep a man and woman. I take a step forward. A bleat pierces the air. I spin to my right and see two sheep tied to a post in the ground, then look back to the humans. They remain asleep. I have never liked sheep.

I walk past the fire and stand at the humans' bedside. They wreak. Mainly the man for he sweats in his sleep. But the woman too, as most humans do. On the ground within arm's reach of the man lies an iron dagger. It would make this easier but I will not have the humans think one of their own was responsible for this. No, that will not do.

With a thrust, I drive my fist into the man's head and feel his skull crunch beneath it. The bed shakes wakening the woman. As she shoots up, I grab her head and twist it around, hearing her neck snap. Her lifeless body collapses back beside the man and I walk out of the home straight to the next.

The village is small, comprising of only six homes and a larger longhouse for the jarl. It does not take long until the jarl's home stands as the last house with living humans yet inside. Upon entering, I see that it is not much different than the others, but this certainly is the jarl's home. Many furs line the ground, the walls, and two benches on either side of a well-constructed table. An axe and a shield stand propped against a wall as well as a leather helmet. On the other end of the home is a rather large bed covered with many furs, seemingly a lot more comfortable than the other beds in this village. On this bed lies the jarl on the left, his wife on the right, and a child in between.

I approach the bed and see that the child remains no

older than eight years. His shaggy blond hair matches his father's. I wonder what it feels like to fall asleep at night knowing your father will be there in the morning. Loki never was. He was not there to teach me to hunt or build or work. I wonder what it is like for this child. I am sure he awakens and his father commands him do his chores. Shovel the animal shit out of the house, refill the troughs, fetch more water from the river, and then return for breakfast. Perhaps then he and his father would go work the farms with the farmers or maintain their small boats with the shipwright. Perhaps his father brings him on hunts and teaches him how to fight.

The boy's eyes open and he screams. Both his parents jump up. I see a glint of light come from the right. I reach out and grab the woman's hand clutching a dagger and twist her wrist. I break her neck before the dagger hits the ground.

The jarl had scrambled out of bed and just retrieved his axe. I turn to face him, now standing on opposite sides of the fire burning in the middle of their home. His son remains on the bed clutching onto a sheepskin, cowering behind it yet watching me with frightful eyes.

With a growl, the jarl steps forward and swings his axe at me. I step aside and he swings once more. Upon his next attack, I move against him and grab the wooden shaft, ripping the axe from his grip. I toss the axe aside. The man now stands at the foot of the bed, between his son and me.

"Do what you will with me, kill me if you must, but do not harm my son. He has done you no harm."

"Why would I grant you such a mercy?"

"Surely you would not harm a defenseless boy. It is not a mercy upon me, but upon him. Spare his life, I beg."

"Nay, it is a mercy upon you for you would die knowing your son will live on in your stead. What is it you fear, human? Do you fear the death of your son? Why would you fear his death and not your own?"

LEGEND OF FENRIR

"I do not fear death for I will find my way to Valhalla. My son has yet to live his life. I know not why you come with intentions to kill for I have never once met you but I ask you to let my son live."

"To Valhalla you say?" The word burns on my tongue. The jarl remains silent. "Answer me this: why should your son live on while mine could not? Why should I grant your son the mercy of life while mine were dealt the punishment of death?"

He offers no answer. I lunge forward, latching onto his tunic. He attempts to offer struggle in futile attempt. I hit him twice in the face and throw him to the ground while the screams of his son fill our ears. Reaching down, I grab hold of the jarl, pick him up, and slam his face down on the bed. I tug on his hair and show him his son.

"Look at your son. Is he alive?" Confused at my question, he fails to offer an answer. I tug harder. "Is he alive?"

"Yes."

"Then you will die without seeing his death. That is the mercy I grant unto you." I throw him backwards on the floor and drive my foot down upon his face, crushing his skull. The next instant, I feel a stabbing pain in my back. I spin around and see before me the boy with his mother's dagger in his shaking hand. Touching my back, I feel a small laceration. It is a good thing the boy has a weak hand.

I slap the dagger from his hand and he cowers beneath me. Yet, I cannot move my hand against him. A human he is but indeed, this boy has done no wrong to me. This boy stands as my siblings and I did back in Asgard. We lived our lives causing no harm. And then the Æsir came and deemed us worthy of punishment and death. I may hate the humans like the Æsir hate the Jötnar, and I may deem them expendable in my desire for revenge, but I will no longer take their children from them. Like Sköll and Hati were taken.

I leave the boy and his village behind as the sun begins

PETER CURSON

to brighten and begin my journey westward anew. Thoughts of worry enter my mind for if the boy leaves the village, he can alert others to what has happened. That is, if he knows the way. I have not seen any sign of other people in days so I doubt he would survive the journey to wherever the next town may lie. No, he will stay. All of the livestock have been left to him; he will have plenty of food to last him until someone finds the village. And what then will he tell them? A man did this. It foils my plan, but one day when I face Odin once more and for the last time, I can stand all the taller knowing I did not condemn innocent children to death for my own gain.

These feelings of worry soon leave my mind for I soon begin to thirst for blood once more. I have whet my appetite on the lives of the humans, those Odin professes to watch over. And I want more. Kára was right: hate is a beast with a hunger that cannot be satisfied. But I like this beast hungry.

Three villages next and I still have not found my way back to that town upon the lake where I found the shaman. Surely by traveling west I move in the right direction. However, how far north am I—or south? Could I have missed it? If so, I would soon arrive in the land of Norvay which would not help me for only King Alf's shamans have been handed down the runes and have practiced using them. Maybe that is what I should then do: find the head shaman himself. If he remains close to the King, it will not be hard to find him. Yet, that carries extreme risk on its own. Not only will the King's armies be ready to protect him, the gods surely will have their eyes upon him. I doubt I could venture within a day's walk of him without being noticed by Huginn and Muninn, Geri and Freki, or one of the gods.

In fact, I feel slightly uneasy that I have come this far without any sight or sound of my pursuers. It is out of the

LEGEND OF FENRIR

realm of possibility that they called off the hunt. Perhaps it is a fortunate string of coincidence that has led me from their eyes, that my movements across Svealand slip past theirs. Or perhaps they know of my location and trail me, waiting for the opportune moment to strike. It is possible that the ravens fly at a distance out of earshot and low to the trees. Yet I have spent many nights asleep. Why wait longer to waylay me and allow me time to sack more villages? Nay, I still have some time yet to find my way. And all I can do is keep my feet moving.

I cannot help but fantasize about the days ahead. Battle and war is something I have not fully experienced but has long since laid at my feet. Finally I tread on war's path. To Hélheim I go to prepare the armies of the dead and then to Jötunheim. My homeland. And there to I will go to prepare and raise up the Jötunn army alongside my wife. Never again will I have to conceal my power. Never again will I face punishment for what I am—for who I am. My people will receive me. They will rally around me. They will fight by me.

I can see it now: I stand at the forefront of the Jötunn host. Hyrrokkin stands beside me and Jormungand too. And there alongside us is Hél, leading her hordes, mindless and rampant. We will stand before the very walls of Innangard and the Æsir will cower at our might. Our march will cause the ground to tremble. Our battle cry will shake the city walls. And on that fated day, the Æsir will face our wrath.

A joyous thought indeed. One to take my mind off this trek through Svealand's landscape and forests. It is long and without any happenings to keep my mind occupied. Such were the days when traveling from the East when first setting off to find my sons. However, Midgard was still new to me. The lands changed and I encountered new animals and plants and I always had Sköll and Hati to keep my mind busy—which was not always pleasant in those days.

PETER CURSON

But now, what new sights are there? I have spent quite a long time now traveling in Svealand and it has become all so common. The lands here look as it did three days past, just as it did even in Gautland. Trees cover the land, only broken up by the many, many lakes strewn about. Yet above all else, the isolation affects me most, though the isolation is not as bad now as it was during the winter in those desolate lands east of here. Indeed I am still on my own but knowing the humans are around, that their villages are close, brings me some sense of comfort—that I am not in complete isolation. And soon, I will arrive at the next village. But before I kill all the people, I will find out where in Svealand I am.

"Who are you?" he stutters as he struggles to speak between shallow breaths. I do not blame him; I too would struggle to breathe if I were the town's jarl and I stood among all my slaughtered villagers facing the person who did it with his bare hands.

"King Alf," I reply, causing his face to scrunch in confusion. I roll my eyes. Humans are dense. "What name does this village go by?"

"Its name is Oförtjänt."

"In which direction is Hämnd?"

"I do not know a village named Hämnd."

I break my stare from the jarl and look around at the mangled corpses and the pools of blood surrounding them holding out my hands as if to say, 'Look what I did.' He gets my meaning for his mouth opens and closes like a fish out of water for a moment as he tries to find his words.

"It is not that I will not tell you, it is that I cannot. I am not well-traveled. Gaidar, that man there, was the one who traveled on my behalf," he says pointing to a man whose arms I tore from their sockets and used to club his brother to death.

"There is a market town I found during my travels," I

LEGEND OF FENRIR

say. "It serves as a waypoint between Svealand and Norvay, located upon a large lake."

"Karlstad, you speak of Karlstad. A market town on the shore of a large lake, yes? It stands a six-day journey southwest upon horseback."

I turn and point southwest to be sure. He nods his head and stares at me with frightened anxiousness. I advance towards him.

"No!" he shouts, backing away whilst tripping upon the bodies of the people he used to know. "Please, I beg spare me! I have done you no wrong and I have helped you all that I could. Why must you do this?"

I sigh. This is why I do not wish to speak to my victims, especially humans. Being so pathetic, their blubbering has an irritating way to delve into my insides, making me pity them all the more. "Perhaps I should grant you mercy this day."

"Many thanks. Many, many thanks," he repeats as I reach down to the ground and pick up an axe. I throw it to his feet, which shuts his mouth quickly. Like an animal in the wild, he realizes that he has but two choices when faced with a predator: fight or flee. He knows in his heart he will die no matter his decision, but one option leads him to Valhalla and the other to Hélheim. Dying as a warrior will grant him admission to Odin's hall and that is the mercy I will grant him this day. His face hardens and he understands the gift I have given him.

He takes up his weapon and charges at me. I dodge his first swing, and his second. It is not difficult to out maneuver him; he is not an experienced warrior. Upon his sixth swing, I see his arms losing their strength and their aim. He over extends on his seventh swing but instead of dodging, I thrust out my forearm aiming for the shaft. It splinters in two. Grabbing hold of the broken handle, I rip it from his hands and he falls to his knees.

PETER CURSON

Between heavy pants he finds the air to ask, "who are you?"

I step up to the jarl and take hold of his hair in one hand. "Ask Odin when you see him." I bring my arm back and thrust the splintered handle into the jarl's widened eye, breaking through the back of his skull. His body falls to the ground and I make my way southwest.

There is nothing like turning from a battle as the victor. When the thrill of the fight fades from my beating heart, my mind is left content. Of course I outmatch the humans, especially for such small villages holding no strong warriors, but I stand a little taller after each victory. When before have I rose victorious in battle? In the days I lived in Asgard and before Thor's sons waylaid us on the road, I only fought with Jor and Hél. Those were not true contests of strength or fighting prowess. Then came our revenge on Modi and Magni in the streets of Bærin. We won that fight. But then the High-Æsir arrived at our doorstep.

No victories I found thereafter until I arrived on Midgard and saved the people of Xwayxway from their enemies. In Asgard, Týr subdued me outside my old home. Odin barely broke a sweat when we battled in the arena at my trial. I could not best Thor in the courtyard outside Valhalla. I also could not contend against the throngs of the dead in Hélheim when I advanced upon Hél's castle. Nor could I defeat Heimdall when attempting escape to Midgard.

I have come far since those days. The freedom I have here on Midgard has allowed me to strengthen and hone myself. I have grown and so too has my power. As I now stand, I surmise I could contend with Vidar or Vali, or even Týr. Odin and Thor stand the largest obstacles before me. Though, I do not fret. If I have grown this strong from roaming Midgard, I will surely thrive when in Jötunheim and become

LEGEND OF FENRIR

stronger than I ever deemed possible. That day is not so far away. But first, I must make it to Karlstad.

    I smell smoke. It has only been two days since I left the last village behind. The jarl told me it is a six-day journey by horse to reach Karlstad, which means about three days for me while shifted. I have not yet come far enough to have found Karlstad, nor do I smell the lake. This means another village lies close by. Such is well; I can confirm the jarl's directions. I do not believe he lied to me, but a human will do anything to escape death, including lying in hopes I would simply leave him be.

    Turning my head to face the brisk morning breeze, I gain my bearing and follow the smell of burning wood. Surprising it is to smell smoke without sight or sound of the village, but it is not thick enough to warrant alarm. Perhaps the village hosts a feast. How lovely! The smell of cooking meat will soon accompany the smoke and whet my appetite. Now I will have food prepared for me to rid my tongue of the taste of human blood.

    My fantasies are cut short when I near the forest's edge. The village, now in earshot, is full of men dressed for battle. They gather around many fires cooking their morning meal before setting out. Where they set out to I do not know. It certainly spikes my curiosity. I shift so as to not alert the warriors and sneak to the forest's edge. They prove too far to pick out any discernable words. I kneel down in the dirt and watch the men and look over the village. A hundred fighting men, not counting the elderly, women, and small children. However, there stand only enough homes to house a couple dozen families. Most of these warriors have come from different places, presumably moving through the region from town to town collecting more men as they go. They have been called to war. And I cannot help but think it is because of me.

PETER CURSON

"Do not move!" a voice calls from behind me.

Damn my hearing! No human has ever managed to sneak up on me like this. I listen intently now and hear two bows being drawn from the left and right of the man who spoke.

"Stand up slowly and turn to face me," the man commands, thankfully not loud enough for the other warriors to hear.

I do as he says and slowly stand. I turn to see three humans much like those in the village: armed and ready for battle. Two men hold bows strung and at the ready while the man in the center holds a small doe over one shoulder and an axe in his free hand. His blond hair is tangled and knotted from his hunt and the stench from his body is utterly fetid. Nearing mid-age, he stands tall and bears broad shoulders with large arms, but his belly has seemed to grow large as well. It shows bravery he does not stand at the ready against me, or folly. But then again, he could not possibly conceive the power I hold.

"What is your business here?" he asks.

"I come to join your ranks."

"Is that so? Naked?" I did not think of taking along any clothes from any of the previous villages. I did not think I would have shifted back to this form. But he continues. "I do not know many warriors who would march to war without gear or weapon. Or perhaps you do not wish to support us in arms, but support us in other ways. Look, the *ragr* boy comes already presenting himself before us!"

"It would do you much harm to spout that word without knowing who you use it upon," I reply. "Choose your next words wisely."

The man laughs. Not good for him. "Surely this *ragr* fool does not threaten me!" He drops the doe and advances

LEGEND OF FENRIR

to me, within my arm's reach, but I restrain myself for my curiosity begs me leave him be in order to see what he wishes to do next. "Is that what you do, boy? Do you threaten me?"

"I am surprised you prove intelligent enough to arrive at such a challenging conclusion."

He laughs again, louder than before. He brings his face close to mine taking in a large breath before shouting "*Holmgang!*" as loud as he can, catching the other warriors' attentions. And they start to cheer. The man points his sword towards the town, motioning for me to move. I stand my ground.

"Will you not fight me? Will you not accept my challenge?"

I turn back to the village and see the warriors and villagers have created a small circle in the field with an opening. They shout at us to enter. It seems this man has challenged me to a duel. I smile wide—my first genuine smile in quite some time.

FOURTEEN

The crowd erupts both in cheer and laughter as I leave the forest and walk to the circle of people. The warriors shout jests and insults at me but they make me smile all the more. I enter the circle and find it small, measuring only several paces across. Not a lot of space for maneuvering. It seems their duels do not test true fighting ability, only sheer strength.

My challenger enters the circle and the crowd closes behind him. He hands off his axe and is given a sword and shield by one of his comrades. "Someone offer this fool their sword and shield!" he calls.

A man to my right shoves a shield into my chest and tosses his sword to me. I fit the shield on my left arm and hold the sword in my right. I have not fought with sword and shield before. An uneasy, but exciting feeling pulses through me. The thrill of a new challenge. He stands experienced in fighting with sword and shield but I stand far stronger. And I will

LEGEND OF FENRIR

prove quicker; not only is my challenger large and fat in stomach, this sword and shield hold nearly no weight in my arms. Hah, let the fight begin!

"Swords and shields only," the human says, stating the rules. "Stepping outside of the circle serves as a forfeit, as does fleeing. Victory is achieved when one fighter kills or otherwise incapacitates his enemy."

"Do you wish to talk or to fight?" I shout. The crowd cheers in response. The man screams and runs at me.

He begins his attack with a thrust of his shield following immediately with a slash of his sword. I block shield with shield and deflect sword with sword. His torso stands open and I thrust but he is ready for it. He parries my sword to the side and stabs forward, slicing my forearm before I bat it away with my shield and push him backwards with it. He has drawn first blood.

Keeping his momentum, he slashes down from behind the comfort of his shield. I block it with my own, and the other two subsequent slashes. I keep my shield raised close to me but instead of another slash, he stabs the shield, forcing it to smash my jaw. He seizes the moment and aims for my head. I duck and thrust my shield forward, pushing him back. With his arm still over me, I drop my sword and shield and grip his arm near the armpit. Rising to my feet, I swing him high in the air and drive him into the ground behind me.

My opponent wobbles to his feet as I reclaim my sword and now I seize the moment. I unleash a flurry of slashes upon the man who struggles to block the attacks. The impact of my strikes vibrates through his body, weakening him immensely. And in this moment, I see the realization of fear in his eyes.

As I lift my sword for another strike, he raises his shield and charges me. I plant my rear foot at the last moment and he crashes into me. He fails to move me as if crashing into

PETER CURSON

a stone wall. I push against his shield with my left hand, sending him stumbling backwards. I slash down at his shield, knocking it from his grasp. I swing at his sword and it twists out of his hand.

"Mercy!" he cries but he shall receive none.

I slice his right arm off at the elbow, and his left at the shoulder. I hack off his leg, causing him to fall, and as he does I swing upwards slicing his neck from his shoulders. With a shout, I plunge the sword through his chest and into his heart.

I regain my posture to a silent crowd. They clearly did not expect me to win. Are they now silent with shock, or with anger over the death of one of their own? I look over the faces of the warriors surrounding me. They harden with each passing second. They close their ranks tighter and take up their shields. Swords are drawn. Axes stand at the ready. Spears aim at me.

Now the real fun begins.

I sprint forward, crashing into a man whose axe was not at the ready. He falls back into the man behind him and I push them through the crowd, catching a couple punches and slices from swords. I thrust the man in my grasp to the ground and exit the circle, quickly checking over my wounds. Nothing serious. An arrow flies past my head. I spin and instinctively dodge a second arrow while I witness the small army of soldiers charging for me. I smile wide for all to see and fall forward, shifting as I do.

My front paws land on the ground and the army of men stop as though they were about to fall off a cliff. But they do not look down in shock, but up at me. The fright in their eyes, the fear in their screams, oh they never fail to delight me. But they do not run. One of the men calls to the rest to rally on him and to take down the beast. This truly is a brave bunch. Or foolish. I still have not made up my mind. Alas, they charge once more. Arrows from a dozen archers behind their lines

LEGEND OF FENRIR

attack me but do not fly fast enough to penetrate my hide. Their craftsmanship still has a way to go yet. If those were Æsir bows and arrows, I would sooner be dead.

    I sprint towards the warriors and lower my head with jaws open and tongue salivating. They part down the middle so I choose the right side and snap my jaw. A hearty mouthful, three men by the feel. I chomp down, the overhanging limbs and other body parts falling from my mouth falling as I do. With a swing, I rear my head and toss the remaining body parts overtop of the army now regrouping.

    Now I stand between the archers and their fellow men. Arrows stream through the air aimed at my head as I stomp and trample the archers one by one. One archer proves smarter than the rest and aims for my ankles, shooting an arrow as I crush one of his comrades. The arrow pierces with a sting. He is the next to die.

    As I kill the last archer, the warriors come upon me all at once. I suffer from the slash of a sword and the swing of an axe before I maneuver out of their reach. I circle around them, rounding them up like sheep. Some attempt attack so as to not be caught in my snare but it only shows the rest of the dwindling army the agony of being eaten alive. After the dozen or so men die in fruitless attack, I round up the rest into a cluster and sprint without hesitation. Some run away but others press attack shouting their collective war cry to strengthen their resolve in the face of death. We collide. I trample over them down the middle without issue. The ones I miss on the sides attack my flank as I pass by. Slashes. Hacks. Stabs. Pain.

    I smash through their rear ranks and spin around. Over half of their numbers lie dead or heavily wounded. I check my body. A small trickle of blood runs down my front right leg. The pain is minimal. To test the damage, I place my weight on the leg. The pain increases only marginally—I am still in this fight. One more assault and this battle will be over.

PETER CURSON

The humans spread out across the field wide enough so as to not be caught in one attack but close enough where all could collapse upon me should I attack any of them. Smart. But it will not save them. I dash forward, straight for the center of their group but then dash left, crushing their left flank before the others could react. Keeping my body low, I twirl on the spot, knocking a handful of warriors over as I reorient myself. The humans rally behind one of their heroes and charge towards me in a valiant last attempt. Perfect; the battle ends here. I set off with my head low.

My right ear twitches. Heavy footsteps. I turn my head to look but a severe force smashes into my side, knocking me to the ground. I roll to the side and clamber to my feet.

Týr stands before me.

"Escape this place at once!" he shouts to the humans. They do not listen but stare in dumbfounded wonder at the man who knocked me over. "Go!" he shouts louder than thunder and they turn tail from one of their gods, fleeing into the forest.

Týr faces me. "Fenrir, stop this!"

I look over his shoulder. He is alone. I spin around to face southwest but he calls out after me. "Do not run! You are surrounded; there is no escape. I come as your friend, Fen. I come to stop the killing."

"Where were you?" I shout twirling to face him. "If you have come to stop the killing, then where were you when my sons were killed? I kill for vengeance. If your master had not orchestrated Sköll and Hati's deaths, no humans would have suffered. Do you not know that?"

"Of course I do! I know it in my heart for it tore in two upon hearing of their deaths. Why do you think I helped you that night when you escaped Asgard? I saw what captivity did to you. And I saw your sons' resilience growing up under our rule. If they could have had a life away from strife, I would

LEGEND OF FENRIR

have had it as such. That is why I betrayed Heimdall that night."

"I escaped Asgard to accomplish that same end; I came to find my sons and bring them home to Jötunheim. And that is where I go now. My wife and my people await me. I wish to leave this place behind as well as all thoughts of the Æsir."

"Do not stand there and lie to me. Revenge has consumed you and led you on a path that you cannot turn away from."

I look around while I think, still panting heavily. Týr will not buy into any lies I feed him. He knows me too well and is too intelligent. However, he is as compassionate as he is smart and if I have any hope of escaping a fight with the gods, that is what I must lean on.

"You are right. The need for revenge guided my actions since my sons' deaths, including this very battle. But I indeed tell you the truth: I leave for Jötunheim. Týr, you cannot understand the tragedies I have faced, no matter how hard you try. You do not know what it is like living in a world that condemns you. You do not know what living in captivity does to you. You know freedom. I do not. I never have. That is why I make for Jötunheim: I want to be free from pain, free from torment, and free to do as I will."

He gazes into my eyes with the same compassion I hoped to see. However, he exhales deeply and fortifies his stature. "I believe you, I truly do, and as sure as my heart does sway, my will does not, nor does the will of the master whom I serve. The judgement Odin passed on the day your siblings were banished still holds and remains violated. Further yet, since that violation you have committed countless more offenses against Odin and his law. Fenrir, unless you surrender yourself to me, I will force you into submission."

I sense the difficulty in his chest with those last words

PETER CURSON

but he stands firm as my enemy. Movement catches my eye. From the forest all around appear the gods. Thor and his sons reveal themselves behind me in the direction I wish to flee. The odds look grim.

"Why would I go with you now as a captive only to be executed in front of the Æsir as a corrupt Jötunn? Tell me why I should not rather fight you here so that I may meet a worthy end?"

"Because I do not wish to execute you," a voice says. Behind Týr a figure emerges from the trees. Odin. He walks across the field calmly, his footfalls gentle and silent. What surprises me is that he does not carry his spear with him. He approaches us and when he takes his spot next to Týr, I truly sense no indication of aggression or attack. But I will not believe it.

"Surely the Allfather, wisest of all beings, could craft a better lie than that," I reply.

"No lie has passed my lips. If I still wished that end, we would have spent this time fighting instead of speaking."

"Then what has changed your mind from such a glorious event?"

"You have proved your strength has grown immeasurable, Fenrisulfr. If I may confide in you, it scares me. I know, just as you do, that if you battled with us upon this field you could slay one, maybe two of us before we subdued or killed you. I am sure you have already settled your mind on such an end, placing me between your jaws before my sons could take you down. That is an end I wish to avoid. Thus, I sent Týr to speak with you. Now I ask you to submit willingly." He reaches into his cloak and reveals a coil of what looks to be silk ribbon. "Allow me to tie this around your limbs as a fetter so that we may bring you back to Asgard safely and I will prove to you the truth of my words."

The fetter looks as though it would come apart in

LEGEND OF FENRIR

Odin's hands if he breathed too heavy upon it. I take a step closer to further inspect it. This is not sane. Why would he bind me with something so odd? I take another step and sniff, faintly smelling the stench of dwarf upon it.

"Nay, you will not bind me with that fetter."

"Surely such a dainty ribbon does not scare you since you have broken free from our largest and strongest chains! We would not be so unwise to attempt to permanently secure you with this. It is only to give you the peace of mind you require to come with us, for if we do attempt to deceive you, then you can simply break free and escape."

"None of this gives me peace of mind." I avert my attention to Týr, looking for a response for how I should proceed. Perhaps the words he spoke aloud were only for Odin's benefit and if there was something more to this, he would silently tell me. But he looks genuine and after holding my gaze for a moment, he nods.

"If you do not wish to kill me, what then do you wish to do? Hold me within your city once again? Banish me to Niflheim's frozen wastelands or Muspelheim's burning plains?"

"I will make my intentions known when back in Asgard. You have but one choice before you, Wolf of Jötunheim: live or die."

I gaze around one more time. The gods surround me. Geri and Freki stalk around the field awaiting my move, snarling angrily for losing me in our last chase. Huginn and Muninn circle above. I escaped them before but now surrounded and wounded, I do not think I could slip from their grasps again. Flight is not feasible. To a wolf, that leaves but one option. But for a Jötunn who wishes to live to see the day Odin is slain and my sons avenged, fight is not an option either. Is my last remaining option really to walk willingly into their thralldom once more?

PETER CURSON

Hyrrokkin, it is in your hands.

"So be it. But before I will allow you to bind me with any fetter, chain, or ribbon, I require a gesture of good faith. One of you must place his hand between my jaws. In this way, you will be sure not to deceive me."

None of High-Æsir stir. Odin and Týr only stare at me. Vidar and Vali do not so much as twitch. Modi and Magni show no outward signs even alluding to their thoughts. Thor looks angry, which is not uncommon nor out of place. He surely exercises great restraint so as to not interject with this negotiation; it is quite the surprise. Turning back to Odin and Týr, they still make no move or speak any words. Which can mean only one thing.

"It is a deception!" I shout.

"Nay, Fenrir," Odin says. "For obvious reasons, my sons do not trust your word that you would not bite their hand at first taste."

"Yet I am to trust your word?"

"I will do it," Týr says, stepping forward. "Fenrir, you know in your heart that you can trust me, and I know that I can trust you not to bite my hand in feeble attempt of escape." The God of War approaches me and extends his right hand—his sword hand.

It seems this is not a ploy. Odin sent in Týr to calm me with words instead of instigating another battle. Thor restrains himself, which he would only do under the direct command of Odin himself. For what other reason would Odin have to hold him back? There is no hope for escape from this field. There is no hope for survival if I fight. Odin does wish me back to Asgard as a captive. For what purpose, I still do not know, but I will have the time to figure that out later if I go with them. The last ray of hope shines from captivity—from knowing that I will remain alive, at least for a while longer. I can find another opportunity for escape, just like that

LEGEND OF FENRIR

night I escaped Asgard across the Rainbow Bridge. And should no opportunity arise, Hyrrokkin will one day come with the Jötnar host along with Hél and her undead hordes. Loki awaits that day in Asgard and if it comes to it, so shall I.

Exhaling sharply, I arch my neck down, open my mouth, and take Týr's hand between my teeth. Now face to face, I stare into his eyes. No deception. No fear. So be it. I clamp down so that he cannot break free of my grasp, and I bring my legs together.

Odin moves to me and secures my front paws with the fetter. Týr's eyes do not waver from mine nor do mine waver from his. In this moment, I remember the day Jor, Hél, and I were captured and taken from our home. On the flight to Innangard upon Thor's chariot, I asked Týr if I could stand and look upon the landscape from the air. It was such a piteous request, yet he took pity on me and allowed me to do such. Later, in the moments before our trial took place, he offered us advice to not resist whatever judgement we would receive. At the time I believed him merely convincing us to conform to their will. Yet it was not so. His pity turned to compassion. As fierce of a warrior as he is, he has always remained compassionate. Just like now.

Odin moves behind me to secure my hind legs and my instincts overwhelm me. Weak fetter or no, it is no easy task allowing myself to be bound. Týr senses my inner strife and still there is no change in his demeanor. He is not worried. And so I must place my trust in him as I once used to. But I cannot trust Odin; I will not allow myself to be tied unless I know I can break the fetter.

Instantly, I pull at the fetter binding my front paws. It does not break. Odin rushes to hold my legs together, holding them within his embrace. My heart explodes with shock and fear.

"Fenrir, stop!" Týr shouts.

PETER CURSON

My instincts take over. I thrash about, trying to break my front legs free of the fetter and my hind legs from Odin's grasp. Neither can be undone. In a matter of seconds, I jump in the air and smash to the ground while Týr screams in pain as he flails through the air with me. I spin and tumble, roll and flail. Odin's grip begins to loosen but the fetter only tightens further.

Another set of hands lays themselves around my legs, and then another as Odin works to tie them. I growl loud and fight against them with all my power, but I feel the fetter tightening around my legs as well. Within moments, the fetter is tied and I can no longer move any of my legs and I fall upon my side, landing in the grass. Týr collapses with me, his arm caught within my teeth. Tears of pain and anguish fall down his face. "Fenrir, I am sorry."

He deceived me!

No!

This cannot be!

My heart beats harder and my head whirls with rage. My vision blurs but I fixate on Týr. His face shows anguish and regret but all my eyes see is an Æsir cur as wretched as his master.

I bite down, my teeth sinking through his flesh and bone. Týr's hand drops into my mouth and a quick spurt of blood trickles over my tongue before he retracts his handless limb. The hand passes over my tongue and into my stomach and I continue to thrash in hopes I can escape my bonds since I cannot break them. To no avail. Odin calls for Thor while Vidar and Vali carry Týr away from my reach.

Thor steps into my view holding Mjölnir. He brings his face close to mine and smiles wide. His hammer sparks. He brings the hammer back and propels it straight for my head.

All goes black.

FIFTEEN

Murmurs. Laughs. My head hurts. I cannot move my legs. Stones scratch my head as I shuffle. I am no longer in the grass field. The smell of the forest is gone. The wind blows. I hear water. Fresh water by its smell. No fish. My stomach hungers. My head hurts more. I open my eyes. Bright light burns my eyes. I close them shut until the pain subsides and squint them until my eyes adjust and my vision clears. Purple flowers wave in front of me. Heather. It has been a while since I have laid eyes upon such flowers. Behind them, I see the water. It reflects the blue sky above as would a rippling mirror. The shallow ripples mesmerize me and I cannot take my eyes from them. The sound soothes me. A weariness overcomes my head and my vision blurs. I force my eyes up and see across the water trees hundreds of feet tall. I am not in Svealand. This looks like… Asgard. My sight fades and all returns to black.

Pounding. Loud pounding. The murmurs are no more

PETER CURSON

but I sense several people standing close. Watching. More pounding. I force my eyes open. It is sunset. A glorious sunset. One I have not seen since my days in Asgard. The blazing sun sets behind a sea of trees rising so high they attempt to stab the clouds. The water remains calm and only flows with the wind, encircling the land on which I stand. I sit upon an island in the middle of a lake. A large boat is moored upon the shore and in front of it stand a cluster of people. I focus my vision. The High-Æsir and their wives. Frigg, Odin's wife, stands tall beside Sif, Thor's wife. They put forth a bearing of strength, but I can sense their fear. Further yet, I see Frey and Freya with their escorts. All silently watch me. I see not Odin, Thor, or Týr.

My head hurts still but I find that my legs do not. They are no longer constricted. I go to move them and find that I can. Instinctively, I come out of my grogginess, rise, and dash forward. I make it two strides before I feel a harsh tug against my body and a tight constricting around my neck. They retied the fetter from my legs and wrapped it around my body and my neck. I turn my head back and see Odin standing close by with Gungnir in hand. He stands beside a massive stone shaped like an upside-down cone thrust into the ground, wider than I am long. At its top stands Thor with Mjölnir in hand. When he sees that I can no longer move, he raises the hammer with both hands and smashes the rock beneath his feet and nails it further into the ground, and with it, I am pulled backwards while the ground shakes from deep beneath us. The ends of my fetter run along the ground to the obelisk and sink down into the earth underneath it. Thor pounds again and again, driving the stone further into the earth until it stands just taller than me. Judging from the rumbles beneath my feet, it must descend hundreds of feet into the ground. I tug against the fetter but the rock does not move and the fetter clings tighter around my body and neck.

LEGEND OF FENRIR

Thor jumps down from the obelisk and walks in front of me with Odin beside him. They stand there as if waiting for me to speak. Rage builds within me once more for I have no words left to speak. They deceived me. Týr deceived me. The cowards! Every one of them! They act pure and righteous but achieve their ends by lies and trickery. The Æsir do not stand for just ideals. The Æsir do not stand higher than the Jötnar. As all beings in the Nine Worlds, they think only of themselves. They lie, cheat, cause war, inflict suffering on those inferior to them. They break trust with those foolish enough to place their confidence in them. They count friends as nothing.

The two gods stand for another moment watching as my fury grows, and finding no words themselves, turn and walk away.

"You have not won!" I shout. "This is not a victory, Odin, you treacherous, one-eyed fool! Go now, and boast of my chaining to your people, but do not claim it a victory, for you only delay your doom. You tie me to this island because you are afraid to fight me. But one day my binds will snap and it will be you whom I seek! Watch for me in the shadows. Listen for me in the woods. One day I will be free and I will summon all chaos upon this land! I took the War God's right hand! You will not withstand the onslaught I unleash. Great disaster will arise. I will go forth with my mouth open wide, my upper jaw touching the sky and my lower jaw against the earth and I will consume all in my path. Trees will shake and burn, mountains will fall, and the stars will swiftly disappear under darkened skies. I will tear apart Asgard to the very gates of Valhalla with the blood of the gods dripping from my claws and flowing from my fangs. You will face my wrath!"

The two gods arrive at their boat and with silent anxiousness, the group boards ready to leave me on this island. My mind escapes me for my rage cannot be undone. I pull against the fetter with all my strength, ignoring the pain, and I

PETER CURSON

pull again. I do not stop. I cannot stop. My fury unleashes taking over my entire body as I flail about. I jump up and down, I stamp and thrash. I roar loud, hearing the Ásynjur shriek with fear. I turn and smash into the obelisk over and over. The pain fuels my rage and I do not want it to stop. I turn my tail to the boulder and pound the ground beneath me, jumping back and forth. Rising inside of me is a strength that I have never before felt.

From the shore I hear heavy footsteps approaching. I turn and behold Týr running from the boat with sword in his only remaining hand. My instincts elude me as my wrath intensifies. Rumbling echoes all around me and amidst my thrashing, I see trees topple. The earth shakes under my paws and I feel a heat igniting within me. I am powerless to subdue it. I plant myself against the ground and howl to the sky as flames burst from my nostrils and my eyes.

Týr jumps into the air with sword raised and lodges it firm into my mouth. The swords tip lodges between my upper teeth and the guard between my lower. He lands on the ground and looks at me with fist clenched. I cannot speak or move my mouth. I stare in hatred at the Ás. After a fleeting moment, he turns to the ship, climbs aboard, and the gods sail to the furthest shore and return to Valhalla.

One day, Odin, you will face my wrath.

EPILOGUE

A screech fills the air. I open my weary eyes and see soaring through the air a large falcon. It perches itself on a tall tree across the lake for a moment and watches me. I have seen this bird before. It takes wing once more, gliding down from the tree and over the water straight towards me. My body is weak and I have not the energy to lift my head from the dirt. The falcon glides just before me, and flaps its wings to land. As it does, its form shifts and there before me stands a man I have not seen for a long time.

My father.

"Finally, I have found you," Loki says. He steps to me and dislodges the sword from between my jaws and I close my mouth with great relief. Once my dry tongue and throat are slick with saliva once more, I speak.

"You have found me. To what end?" I ask.

"For the day you when you break free of this fetter. They would not tell me where you were bound. I have searched Asgard looking for you—every hill and every crevasse."

LEGEND OF FENRIR

"The day I am free? Free me now!"

"Fenrir, it is beyond my strength. Your fetter is chained to a boulder held in place beneath the earth with this obelisk acting as a fastening pin. Thor drove it into the earth with Mjölnir. An ant would sooner free a nail from wood than I this obelisk from the ground. And if you could not break your binding, I surely could not."

I position my head to look behind me and inspect my fetter once again. It still looks like ribbon even as it constricts me harder than steel ever could.

"What is it?" I whimper.

"Its name is Gleipnir—a craft of the dwarves. Odin beseeched the dwarves for their help once you broke free of the Æsir's most formidable chains. The smiths worked day and night. No iron did they use, nor any other substance from the ground. Using their dark magic, they took away from the world six things and used them in forming a fetter that could not be undone: the spittle of a bird, the sinews of a bear, the roots of a mountain, the beard of a woman, the breath of a fish, and the sound of a cat's footfall. It was made to withstand the sands of time. As they raised you in Asgard, they watched in fear. And when you proved their fears valid the day you battled Fafnir and killed Sigurd, they knew they could not allow you to remain free."

It is as I feared. There is nothing I or anyone can do to free me from this insufferable misery.

"Can you not shift down to your normal self to escape Gleipnir?"

"Nay, I have long thought there was magic upon this fetter for it further tightens upon me at any attempt of escape. I fought my mind for many months wondering if it was just my imagination but your words confirm it. If I shift, the fetter will tighten with me and I fear I will no longer be able to shift for it will not give. I am stuck as I am."

PETER CURSON

"It will not be so forever," he says, attempting to assuage my misery. It only worsens it.

"Leave me and let me wait for a death that will never arrive and for a hope that has long since extinguished."

Loki stares at me for a minute longer. Finally, I close my heavy eyes and attempt to sleep, hoping I never again will wake.

He places his hand on my head and from his touch I can sense inner tumult. It is genuine. He rises and in an instant, takes off, the sound of his flapping wings escaping into the distance.

Sköll. Hati. My sons...

Nordic Short Stories

Hereafter follows Peter Curson's Nordic short stories, based on myth or on historical Viking Age events.

The Vagabond is a short story Curson wrote during college in preparation for his novel *Exile of Fenrir*. Thus, there will be many similarities in lines and descriptions. However, *The Vagabond* is its own work and in no way related to the Exile series. Fenrir remains the main character and the story remains told in first-person point of view. However, his fundamental character is very different from what you have just read, as are the other characters. No inferences or parallels can or should be made between this short story and *Exile of Fenrir* or *Legend of Fenrir*. Simply enjoy this work as a new narrative based on an authentic Norse myth.

The Land of Snow and Sorrow is also a college-written short story. This story was written as a way to build and flex Curson's historical fiction muscles in a way to prepare for the writing of *Legend of Fenrir* when Fenrir moves from the fantastical realm of Asgard to the very real and historical Midgard, specifically modern-day Sweden. *The Land of Snow and Sorrow* follows real-life explorers and their horrific tale on a newly discovered land.

The Vagabond

I was only five when the gods looked at me in fear. They feared my strength and my size, what I was capable of, but above all else, they feared my race: the Jötnar. They call us the Chaotic. Because of my anarchic nature and my "ungodly" anatomy, the gods raised me in their home world, Asgard—the pinnacle of beauty and tranquility. They did this to keep me close, never to roam free. In this way, I could be watched. Controlled. Many long years have passed since those days. I can no longer recall my time in Asgard, nor any pleasant memories. I can only remember their treachery as I sit here chained upon this mountain, forever in solitude. Forever isolated.

The hairs on the nape of my neck stand on end and my ears perk forward. Something is near. I sense it. I listen first and then I sniff. The frigid wind is blowing from behind me, carrying the smell of snow and frost, shrouding what is in front. My ears fail me also--nothing in the air but the wind rushing between the mountain peaks. Though winter has fallen upon this land and the sun's warmth rendered powerless, my body remains warm. Cold weakens only my prey.

Whatever is nearly upon me knows that I am here. With my other senses masked, I must rely on my sight. My body remains still, unmoving, as I scan the area in front of me. The rocks have not moved since many moons ago when the sky tore apart with thunder and lightning, sending gales and torrent to reform the land. The frost has also remained untouched. I make two passes with my eyes but see nothing different from how it has always been. So I take one step forward and then another, crunching the frozen ground beneath me. Boulders jagged and tall rise around me, enough to conceal my prey but not nearly enough to conceal me. Natural instincts guide my body. All my senses are honed and though I cannot smell, hear, nor see anything, I lunge. Pain surges through my rear leg as it is sharply strained. I crash to the ground with my leg hanging in the air behind me. I thought I had more room. Nine steps: that is all I have. Scampering backwards, I regain my forward stance but hear something behind the boulder in front of me. A man laughs.

"Reveal yourself, coward!"

The frost crunches under heavy steps and a figure walks out, clothed with many furs. A hood is cast over his head but the frosted ends of his hair flutter, exposed in the wind. A sword hangs strapped on his right hip. I know of only one man who wields a weapon with his left hand: one who no longer has his right.

"Ah, Fenrir, Wolf of Jötunheim!" he says to me. "Here I expected to see you as you once were: large, strong, with fur thick as fog and dark as night. Yet before me, I see a piteous pup starved and defeated. Where are your glaring teeth? Your blackened claws? Your malicious eyes full of bloodlust?"

"Cease your mocking, Týr. Coward you are, for if you took three paces forward, your tongue would share the same doom as your right hand. Why have you come?"

"I felt like going for a short jaunt," the large man replies looking around, though man he is not, rather one of the gods.

"You have come no short distance and, by the looks

of you, have not enjoyed it. If you have come to see if I am still chained here, you will be pleased to see that I am," I say brandishing the fetid chain that secures my leg to this mountain peak.

"I am confident we both know that if you have not broken free from Gleipnir's grip by now, Fenrir, you never will. The dwarves made sure of that."

"You have a bothersome way of avoiding the question at hand. Something must have driven you to leave your utopia to travel to this place. You would not disrupt my endless punishment of solitude if not for some pressing matter."

Týr's face turns rigid but he does not answer. His eyes remain fixed on me, his jaw clenched like his fist. I smell his odor growing stronger as he sweats despite the temperature. It does not take my astute senses to see his anger and his hatred. After all, his bitter right hand has long since passed through my jaws and into my stomach. "Do they still call you 'God of War' back in Asgard despite your loss? Is that why you have come, for revenge and to reclaim your prestige?"

"Neither."

Something is different. The war god always carried himself fearlessly, even when he willingly held his hand in my mouth as Odin, chief of the gods, chained me to this mountain. They assured me it was a game of strength. I had broken free of two chains beforehand, barely flexing my muscles doing so. But this chain, Gleipnir, looking more like a dainty ribbon, set off all my instincts at once. Yet in my folly, I judged it simply as it looked. But before I agreed to this third test, I needed an act of good faith. Thus, Týr volunteered to put his hand in my mouth, knowing full well that the dwarves fashioned this unbreakable chain. Despite all his treachery and deceit, his bravery was true and strong. But now as he stands here, perspiring like a nervous child, I can sense something gnawing at his mind. And now the unknown gnaws at mine. I cannot help but feel a rage build inside of me. My controlled breathing becomes erratic and a growl rumbles from within me. Týr takes a couple hasty steps back and turns to leave without a word. "Týr!" I howl. "Answer me!" I rush forward but Gleipnir holds me back once more. "Curse you! Curse you and Odin the treacherous, one-eyed fool! Should I ever break free of my binding, your deaths will come swiftly under darkened skies!" I pull against Gleipnir and pull again. I do not stop. I cannot stop. My rage unleashes taking over my entire body as I thrash about, causing the boulders to shake and topple. The ground begins to tremble. I rise to my feet and pound the mountain beneath me, jumping back and forth. Rising inside of me is a strength that I have not felt since I was first chained. My instincts elude me as my wrath continues to take control. Rumbling echoes all around me and amidst my thrashing, I see rockslides and avalanches cascade throughout the range. The earth shakes under my paws. But what troubles me most is a long dormant heat igniting within me. I am powerless to subdue it. I stomp against the ground and howl to the sky as flames burst from my nostrils and my eyes.

Evening came quickly. It took until the sun touched the distant peaks until I could reclaim myself. The frost around my seat on this mountain has melted and seeped into the infertile ground. The mountains I have spent years observing have been reformed. Cliffs have crumbled, the ground has shifted, trees have fallen. I cannot explain it, but it makes me irritable seeing something I have grown so accustomed to change just slightly yet so drastically. My rear leg aches while Gleipnir holds strong. I lie on my belly, jaw between my paws, and cannot help but let out a whimper.

The wind subsides as the sun hides behind a distant

mountain, not yet below the horizon. It is in this moment of silence I hear something disturb it. Footsteps. They fall gently upon the ground, and cautiously. After a moment, I catch a scent of he who approaches. I recognize it instantly. It is no man this time. My rage and my hatred are overpowered and a pleasantness engulfs me. My whole being is delighted. I push myself off the ground to witness a woman standing before me, dark-skinned with the essence of fire imprisoned in her eyes.

"I felt the earthquakes," she says. Her voice is soft and her tone gentle, bringing such a pure familiarity I believed to be no longer in the realm of reality. But I hear sorrow in her voice, maybe because of how I now appear.

"I am surprised the mountain still stands," I reply.

"I thought... I am glad you are well, Fenrir." Something troubles her as well. It is unlike her to worry over a concern such as this.

"What disturbs you, Hyrrokkin? You are stronger in heart than I, yet you stand there with a face wrinkled with worry."

"My worries are unfounded. Will you tell me why you shook the earth this day?"

"I will tell you, but first come close; night's chill will soon wrap its fingers around us, a cold you would not survive atop this peak." She moves to me and sits down between my paws just as she used to. I lower to the ground, nesting her between my neck and my shoulder. Her body is as cold as the frost now reforming. "Týr visited me this day, saying nothing, hiding something. He journeyed weeks from Asgard to this mountain to say nothing and leave. Perhaps to check if I am still alive."

"Or if you were still here," Hyrrokkin says timidly.

"What do you know?"

"A rumor to my ears," she starts, "but possibly truth to the gods. A prophecy has been foretold by a spirit from beyond death: come Ragnarök, Fenrir will break free of his bonds and devour Odin."

"Devour?" I say with a laugh. "Well this prophecy truly is an imaginative one."

"Do you not believe it then?"

I have never given much thought to prophecies. They assume Fate is rigid. Absolute. I would like not to believe that Fate destined me to sit atop this mountain for the rest of my days. If it was not for my foolish pride and one faulty decision, my fate would have been different.

"Nay, I do not," I respond. My hope for release diminished long years ago when my memories began to fade. One can only suffer imprisonment so long before all he craves is to be free. I would trade the Nine Worlds to escape from this chain. However, I do not know what would happen thereafter. This prophecy speaks of revenge, but how could I enact such a feat? I have not moved from this place for an uncountable number of seasons and I never will. My body is always pained. My stomach is always empty, craving tastes that I cannot remember. And my mind is always lost. How could I contest the god of gods, despite his half-blind sight, should I ever break free?

She shuffles uneasily within my warm embrace. I feel uneasy also. Could it be because of this prophecy she believes in? Or could it be me? Surely I am not who she remembers; it has been a long time since she last visited me. The wolf who resides in her memories is stronger than I, both in body and mind. Perhaps that is whom she still expected to be chained upon this mountain. Now it seems she cannot adapt to this creature keeping her warm.

"Fen, I am sorry. I must return home." She rises from my embrace and steps away.

"No, I beg, do not leave yet. The loneliness… it is unbearable."

PETER CURSON

"I truly am sorry, Fenrir. Glad is my heart knowing you are safe. Should the prophecy ever come to pass and you break free from your bonds, come find me." She turns down the same path that Týr had taken and soon vanishes beyond the veil of darkness now upon the land. Yet I remain watching, savoring the last remains of her scent in the air. At last, I see two orange flickers down the mountain path as she takes one last look at me, illuminated by the moon's light.

"Farewell, my dear wife."

The wind blows colder as it whispers the tale of the land of snow and sorrow—a tale I know all too well. The wind knows my name. It knows my turmoil. It knows me. But tonight, the wind speaks softly of a new chapter unfolding, a second act in a never-ending tragedy. It talks of destiny laced within clouded riddles. It asks me whether I will conform to Fate's will or bend it to my own. I do not answer.

"Cease your storytelling," I say to the wind, "for my ears are now closed to you."

Yet before my mind passes on, it whispers a single word in my ear as vividly as spoken speech: "Ragnarök!"

I open my eyes and my mind is alert. The night is still and silent. Looking to mid-sky, I see the luminous moon shrouded by blankets of ominous clouds. It comforts me—until I realize I am not alone. To my left a fire has been lit. Oh, how I have missed such a smell. Tending to the small fire is a figure with garments tattered. He has a long white beard untouched by winter's frost and a large pointed hat that hides his face. He uses his large walking stick, made of ash wood from the smell of it, to shuffle the logs in the fire. I sniff for his scent but cannot find one. Paying little heed, I instead watch this vagabond as he tends to his fire. I sense no danger nor any threat. I do not sense anything about him. No menace, no peace. All I can do is watch him as my instincts fail me. Is he even real? Is he a spirit of the past from a time before I was chained here? Or is it I who has finally passed on to the land of spirits myself? Perhaps that is it: a spirit I am, no longer visible to the world.

"Are you hungry?" he asks me. It seems my mind wandered a little too far into the realm of possibilities. "I brought a calf with me. I can roast it if you'd like." In fact, he does not wait for my answer as if he knows my stomach's desire. He grabs a sack and pulls out a calf, fresh by the smell of it. It does not take him long to prepare it and put it over the fire. I salivate instantly.

"Who are you?" I ask.

"There are many questions for you to ask, Fenrisulfr, and that is not one of them."

He knows my name. My birth-name.

"How do you know my name?"

"Many people do. It has become well-known throughout the land after your chaining, especially amongst us wanderers. Indeed, vagabonds only have stories to lend. Further still has become known your prophecy."

As he speaks to me, I pick up threads of wisdom coming from his words, yet my own senses cannot analyze him.

"The prophecy is false," I say. "As you can see, I am stuck on this mountaintop. There is no breaking free from—"

"Gleipnir?" says he. "Yes, the dwarves are an exceptional people indeed."

"Exceptional? Nay, vagabond, they are a people of greed and trickery, puppets to the will of the gods of Asgard. They would condemn another's soul to eternal damnation for a chance to whet their appetite for gold and treasure. I have been to their vast underground world, Nidavellir. An aura of greed lingers in that labyrinth, all the way into the deepest cave. My vision turned into gold and silver, where all things had a shine and luster. My nostrils only smelled wrought metal and my ears only heard the pounding of hammers and pickaxes. If the dwarves are exceptional, they are exceptionally corrupt."

The man makes a noise of understanding but it sounds hollow. "Of course someone in your position, facing the fate you do, would hold the dwarves in such contempt, as I am sure you hold the gods of Asgard. Vengeful you must be towards them."

"I have hated both since before my imprisonment, but my mind is lost to all desires apart from being free. I do hate the gods, but what good is revenge without freedom? That is my only desire, vagabond. As it remains, only one emotion remains yet within me: hatred. And it does not end with the dwarves and the gods of Asgard! The gods of Vanaheim are as intolerable as those in Asgard. Their only forgiving quality is their love for nature. They are in likeness to the elves of Alfheim. If there was one place I could return to, I would choose the world of the elves. Despite those complaisant creatures, ignorant to all that happens beyond their world, I am at peace with them. I have never felt any malice within their lands; I could not even bring myself to become agitated. Whereas now, speaking with you, I can recall everything I hate about them."

"And what about Midgard?" he asks.

I laugh. Midgard, world of the humans. "If ever there was a race more corrupt than the dwarves, it would be the humans. Lustful people they are for all manner of things: riches, vanity, anger, hatred, and desire. Never have I seen a people so divided. The dwarves may desire gold above all else, but they would never wish to destroy themselves over it. Yet the humans... nay. I could only remain in Midgard for but a pittance of time before I was affected. Above all of these humanly desires, I felt the desire for power. The need for it."

The man removes the calf from the fire and walks

over to me. At first, he stays where I cannot reach but after a moment of hesitation, he approaches me. I still sense no malice and my instincts remain quelled. He raises the calf as I slowly rise. Complying with my stomach's desire, I sink my fangs into the meat, instantly tasting its succulent juices as they flow into my mouth. He releases the calf and sits back down by the fire. If not for my hunger, I would savor this meal, but instead I swallow it whole.

"Why have you come, with food for me no less?"

"Curiosity," he replies. "It seems I have learned something about you, Wolf of Jötunheim: you, your very being, are influenced by your environment. You are susceptible to those around you and are altered according to their own selves. You saw in shades of silver and gold with the dwarves, you were at peace with the elves, and felt a lust for power with the humans."

His words open my mind like floodgates. Could this vagabond, who has conversed with me for only a short while really be correct? Even now, I think to earlier with Týr, the god of war. It was only then when my hidden flame was ignited. When Hyrrokkin was here, I was calm, feeble, yet uneasy as she was. And for the countless years gone by, my mind has been lost.

"Now I have but one question for you," the vagabond says to me. "What do you feel right now?"

With him? It is a simple question yet I can find no sort of answer within my mind. Why is it so troubling?

"I feel… order—that everything is as it should be."

The man nods to himself.

"Except," I say, his ears perking, "except for one gnaw at my mind that I cannot seem to place. Is it the fear of the unknown? No. Perhaps it is curiosity. Yes, the need for knowledge."

I see a small grin cross his face in the firelight. "Very

PETER CURSON

well. Sleep now, Fenrir; your weariness shows."
As he speaks these words, sleep comes upon me. I do not resist, feeling no danger with him nearby. I allow my fatigue to subdue my consciousness and I fall into slumber.

  I wake to the earth shaking violently beneath me. My instincts flare all at once. The night has passed. The fire is out. The vagabond is gone. My ears fill with the rumbling of rockslides and avalanches. The mountains around me begin to crumble while the valleys split open consuming the falling cliffs. I look to the sky and see the sun and moon side-by-side, traveling together across the sky faster than they should. Baffled by this sight, I stare on and hear two loud noises coming from the sky: howls from wolves. In an instant, the sun and moon disappear and their light diminishes and all turns to darkness. But the all-consuming shadow lasts not, for another light comes upon the land from the south. I gaze to the horizon and see flames spreading like wildfire many leagues into the air, painting the lands with an orange tint. Next, I hear a horn louder than all others call from the north—from Asgard. This is it, the end of days. Ragnarök has come. The prophecies of old are unfolding: the devouring of the sun and moon, the flames from the World of Fire engulfing all things, the god Heimdall signaling the end of time with his final horn blast. Only one prophecy remains to unfold.

  I turn quickly and witness Gleipnir upon the ground shattered. It cannot be. Are my eyes cheated? I brush my nose along my leg and feel no coldness. I sniff and smell no stench of dwarf. I take a step away. Then again. Again. And again until I find myself at the ninth step and as the world begins to collapse around me, I take the tenth step. My leg is released.

  I am free.

  With my tail wagging fiercely, I sit down at that tenth step and gaze out upon the land. The towering flames rage ever onward, engulfing the lands which have embraced me as their own—the lands which I have longed to depart. The glaciers and avalanches have melted into tidal waves crashing into the valleys below, submerging the tallest of trees. The beasts of the land attempt to flee yet only the birds can escape. The snow around me begins to melt from the vast heat of the approaching inferno as the last horizon falls. True doom has begun. And I am joyful. I am free.

Now, it is time to be rid of this place. With one last glance, I revel at the utter destruction. But at last, I turn away. Beside the shards of my fetid chain lay a staff—the vagabond's walking stick. Runes pulsating a mystic blue light were carved along its shaft. It was the vagabond. He freed me. I look out upon the land and see atop one of the few mountains still standing the vagabond upon an eight-legged horse. He lifts his head to me and that is when I see he is missing one eye.

The Land of Snow and Sorrow

A chill slithers up my spine as we hike. It is cold here but it deters us not. Adventure is in our hearts and discovery before our eyes. However, I regret that we have arrived here so late into Autumn. Summer's warmth is most needed and winter's deathly grasp is not far from us. We must find a place to settle if we are to survive the winter. But for now, we three men walk the paths of history as we do something none but our ancestors have been able to do: discover. Once my comrades and I mount this hill, we will have sight over all the land. This new land. The land west of the sea.

"Autumn is colder here than back home," Herjolf says. It is just like him to complain about the cold. He complained about it when we departed Norway, he complained about it in the Faroe Islands, and he complained about it all the way across the sea.

"I am curious; is that what you will talk about upon our return?" Faxe asks. "I will boast with stories of adventure and of a land now discovered—the land only we have stepped upon! It seems all you will do is tell them how cold you were. I have always known you were not strong enough to be a true

Norseman." Indeed, Faxe is stronger in arm and in heart than Herjolf, but if it were not for Herjolf's skill upon the open sea, we would never have survived the treacherous journey. And Herjolf is quick to proclaim this very argument.

"Quiet, both of you," I command. "Why do you two squabble of the future and talk about home when we tread upon undiscovered land? Come; let us bear witness to this beauty in its entirety."

With the sea to our backs, we mount the hill and gaze upon a splendorous landscape. Such vibrant colors! Sloping mountains wind their way to a mossy grassland that stretches to our feet. Glaciers feed cascading streams that meet with the rivers from the sea, creating lakes that paint the ground like a spider's web. A cluster of rocks wrapped in blankets of moss decorates the field below us, and behind them lay a bed of springs with steam rising from their surface, covering the area in a delicate haze. The ocean smell is coupled with refreshing, crisp wind sent from the mountains to greet us. I fill my lungs with this air never before tasted and cannot help but laugh in true adoration.

"The land welcomes us with open arms, Floki!" Faxe says to me with a smile so pure.

"And we receive her embrace," I say. Even Herjolf is laughing with us. Without word, Faxe runs off down the hill towards the cluster of boulders. Herjolf follows. Yet I remain to watch the spectacle before me unfold. We are finally here.

As the thought to descend the hill enters my mind, I feel a frigid gust of wind circle me. It lasts not a second but as the gust drifts away, I hear what sounds like a shrill voice escape into the distance. I move not and listen. Now all is silent except for the sound of the sea, the rivers before me, and my comrades who are shouting at one another. With a shake, I clear my head and run after Herjolf and Faxe.

The other two have already gone ahead as I enter the

cluster of boulders, taller than any man, wondering how they came to be here lifted up like mountains for the bugs of the dirt. I place my hand upon a boulder. It is cold and rough even against my ship-worn hands. Despite all my awe, it is only now when the impact of our discovery hits me. Each night of our journey, I have dreamt of this place, whether it would have tall mountains with jagged peaks like Norway or blissful, rolling hills like the Highlands of Scotland. Would it be a place of innumerable lakes like Sweden or of vast forests like Finland and beyond? But now as I stand here gazing at the droplets of water hiding within the beds of moss, this all becomes real. Never could my mind create such beauteous detail in something so ordinary.

"Floki!" It is Herjolf.

His shout is followed by a horrendous shriek that ceases in a gurgle of agony. By instinct, I draw my sword. Sprinting towards the sound, I navigate between the boulders nearly tripping over my own feet. I step out from behind a boulder and see a sword rush towards my head. I deflect it with my own and grab the attacker's arm. It was Faxe.

"Floki, my apologies! I did not know it was you."

I grunt and shove him backwards. This is where I heard Herjolf's shout. We stand at the edge of a clearing within the boulders. And that is when I see him. Herjolf is sat at the foot of a boulder hunched over himself, his blond hair hanging in front of his face. A sword rests in his unclenched hand. He is still. I run to him and lift his head. His mouth gapes open, the hilt of his dagger lodged within it.

Instantly, I spin and hold out my sword towards Faxe. "What have you done!"

"This was not of my doing; you are brothers to me! Floki, turn away your sword for we must not be alone!"

He may be correct. I do not wish to believe Faxe would commit such a crime but I will not risk my life on such a belief. Before I can respond, the sound of rushing wind meets my ears flowing between the rocks from all around us. As before, a frigid gust circles me and I hear a screech that pierces my ears—like from one of those possessed witches of the South. This wind is not natural.

"Run!" I shout and slash at the air before me. "Get to open ground!" Faxe disappears behind a boulder and I run after him. He is several strides ahead of me and I struggle to follow as he darts around each boulder. The wind chases us, shrieking from behind, in front, and from all around. A gust collides with me as though it was a bear and I crash hard into a boulder. I push off it and sprint away. I cannot fall. I will not die here. At first, I could hear the sound of Faxe's footfalls but now they are lost to me as the wailing and the wind drown out all other sounds. Suddenly, something latches onto my wrist and pulls me sharply backwards but I see nothing as something constricts my arm. I slash at the air in front of my hand as if there was an invisible arm there but I am not released. The shrieking ceases and the unseen claw pulls me closer. The wind seems to converge just in front of my face and it begins to whisper. It soothes me. My fear is multiplied yet my muscles relax and all tension releases from my body. I find my arm no longer resisting and my hand outstretched. A tingling sensation moves across my palm like a woman's touch. And here I stand for many moments staring into empty air with sensations of bliss and misery. Death is upon me.

My mind turns to thoughts of my grandfather's stories of Valhalla, Odin's hall, where the spirits of fallen warriors celebrate eternally with the gods. I never believed his stories nor in the gods. I believed only in what I could see. Yet I stand here in the presence of some ethereal being that I cannot see but know that it is there. Perhaps this is a Valkyrie, a servant of Odin sent here to guide my soul to Valhalla. That does not sound so terrible after all.

PETER CURSON

"Valkyrie, take me where you will. I am yours."

The whispering becomes louder and separates into a collection like that of a crowd. Here upon the shores of a land unknown, I depart this world.

"Floki!" An abrasive hold grips me across my chest from behind and hauls me back, breaking me free of the unseen grasp. It is Faxe. He pushes me in front of him, holding me by the fabric of my tunic, and rushes forward, guiding me out of the cluster of rocks.

We escape onto a small field between the rock cluster and the hot springs ahead. The winds subside and all is silent. Faxe and I stand side by side, swords ready, for what seems like half of an hour. Yet all remains still as though nothing ever happened. Faxe shuffles, startling me. His face is painted with anguish and despair.

"Woe unto us!" he cries. "What have we faced here? That was not of this world."

"Could it," I say, hesitating, "could it have been a work of the gods?"

"In what tale of the gods have you heard such a thing happen? Oh, no, woe unto us! Our doom has begun. This was the work of the Christian god punishing us! It is the Christians who speak of their god's invisible power and his wrath. Floki, we are undone."

"Calm yourself! We have not met our doom, nor will we." But how could I make such a statement? Herjolf has met his doom and if it was not for Faxe, I would have met mine. Whatever waylaid us, whether it be the Valkyries or the Christian god, I doubt it is finished with us. I do not mention my thought of the Valkyries. It sounds foolish enough in my head, even though Faxe talks of the Christian god's existence. Yet here we stand in the middle of a field of moss, surrounded by a façade of peace and tranquility, and the only thing that must be decided is where to go next.

"Well we cannot go back that way," Faxe says pointing his sword at the rock cluster.

I look around us. There is no way back to the ship except by way that leads too close to the rocks. To the north, past the hot springs, lay the foot of a mountain. On either side, smaller hills branch out like the arms of a giant, which circle their way around the rock cluster and back behind them where we first began our journey. The safest road lies north of us. We would climb the mountain and to the west until we are hid behind the hills. It should keep us far enough away from the rocks and hopefully give us a view of the rest of this land.

After telling Faxe, he looks at me and his expression asks the very question on my mind: what if it happens again? I cannot give an answer. No answer exists. I clasp his shoulder and squeeze it reassuringly. "We press on, Faxe. No other option lay before us. Better to fight and fall than to live without hope."

We pass by the first hot spring. The water, a vivid and musky blue, is still with a delicate steam rising from its surface. The springs are large, having narrow paths above the water that weave in between each spring. We gladly welcome the warmth but the cool breeze is ever piercing, creating a rather odd and inconsistent temperature between too cold and too warm. Oh, how I crave a warm bath. My body has not unstiffened since the first night upon the sea. Though, these springs seem too hot and would sooner burn us than soothe us.

We march in silence upon the rocky paths wondering about what had befallen us. I do not even revel in the sight of the world around me. The mountains no longer hold any splendor nor do the springs around us any serenity. All I see before me is the path in which we must take to escape this forsaken place. We were supposed to discover this land, find

PETER CURSON

a place to settle, make it our own. Now one of us lies dead without hopes of a funeral. Herjolf did not deserve such a death. Nor do we. Woe unto us indeed.

Faxe stops. He reaches for his sword. Reaching for mine, I look around but see nothing. More importantly, I hear nothing. It must be paranoia gnawing at Faxe's mind. I place my hand on his shoulder about to offer words of comfort when I see the spring before me breakaway as some invisible force glides upon its surface, sending out ripples upon the water in the shape of an arrow directed straight at us. I push Faxe forward but trip over his feet and we fall hard to the ground. A strong force rushes behind us and with it comes a terrible shriek. They are back.

We pick ourselves up and take off down the narrow path. In the water from all around us we see numerous arrows streaming for us. We run harder, dodging the invisible forces, until we come to a fork with multiple paths leading through the springs. We split apart. I take a path to the left and Faxe down the center. This is not happening. Not again! I flee with only the harrowing screams to drive me forward. There are dozens of them. But as I fly past each spring, I see that I near the foot of the mountain. Maybe if we escape the springs, they will not give chase—just as with the rocks. I dodge two more invisible beings and sprint hard. With mere strides before I escape the hot springs, a heavy weight smashes into my arm, pushing me off balance as I run. I am knocked to the edge of the path, running along its corner swinging my arms wildly to keep balance. If I fall, I die. With a thrust, I launch myself into the air and land at the edge of the path beyond the bank of the spring. I brace myself for the worst, but nothing attacks me. Scrambling up, I look to the water and see nothing rushing towards me. I made it.

Faxe has taken a longer path. He runs hard and I see the fright in his face. However, his legs give way and he falls!

I shout his name and take off to help him. But it is too late. An arrow in the water rushes straight for him. Before he can reclaim his stance, he is knocked into the air and splashes into a spring. He resurfaces and screams in pain. He tries to swim for the path but his clothes and weapon weigh him down. In an instant, dozens of arrows ripple through the lake and submerge Faxe into the spring in a violent thrash. Bubbles rise from the water but soon cease, as do the ripples in the water. Within moments, everything is still. Faxe's body does not return to the surface.

The mountain slopes steadily upwards with moss and grass all over. I keep all thoughts of Faxe and Herjolf from my mind. All I must do is make it to the western hills. Then I will be safe. There is no discernable path except for the one I make. And I must walk it alone. All I have is a direction: west. I will make it to the hills. I will make it back to the ship. I will make it home.

For the past hours, I have hiked. The day has grown late indeed; the sun has set beyond the horizon. Alas, I near the zenith of the first hill that adjoins to the mountain side. The ambition of adventure enters my heart again, even if only but a little. In moments, I will be able to see yet more of the landscape. But it excites me not, knowing that I will see what Herjolf and Faxe never will. I walk onward and upward until I reach the top of the hill that joins into the mountain. The land before me, a rocky tundra, goes on to the darkening horizon where yet more mountains rise. I find no more beauty in what I see. Only pain. Without hesitation, I turn southward to begin my journey across the hills back to the ship. It is in this moment when my heart sinks; the unnatural wind meets me once again. I cannot help but fall to my knees in despair. The gusts of wind, beings of their own, circle around me screeching horribly and close in.

PETER CURSON

"What are you?" I cry out to the wind. "Odin? Valkyries? The god of the Christians? Answer me!"

As if the gusts of wind understood me, their wailing stops and their movements cease but I can hear the wind as if several man-sized cyclones roared in front of me. And here I kneel, at the center of a circle of supernatural beings, completely at their mercy. Yet they do not attack.

"What are you waiting for?" Still nothing happens until I see something—a flicker of light in the corner of my eye. When I turn, I see nothing. But then there is another flicker on my other side. And then another one. Finally, I see. From the ground sprout wisps of ghostly light colored a luminous blue. The mists grow and ascend into the air until fifteen transparent ghosts surround me. They grow just taller than myself and in an instant, they take human shape. They whisper. It is of a tongue I do not understand. Suddenly, the whispering hushes and one of the ghosts slowly advances towards me floating upon its own wind.

Still upon my knees, I straighten my back and stare as the being approaches, now directly before me. It moves its hand to my face and grazes it upon my cheek. I feel it. The ghost lifts my chin and I rise to my feet. We are face to face and I stare to where its eyes would be. It takes its hand from my chin, raises it into the air, and places it upon my head. A jolt of energy surges through me and my body seizes into paralysis. I see before me the ghosts vanish and the land suddenly brightens. The sun has resurfaced in the west and soars in the sky backwards, setting in the east in the blink of an eye. And the moon follows. And then the sun again. The clouds fly through the sky faster than my eyes can follow. I begin to see the land become even greener. In a second, rain pours out upon the land but passes by instantly. The days keep passing by faster and faster until the days pass too fast for my vision to keep up with. Now I see the colors of summer turn to spring, then a sheet of snow covers the land, hiding all color with white and black. And then the snow melts and I see summer once more. Then winter. Then summer. And I remain watching the seasons pass before me for what seems like hours until the seasons stop and all I see before me is winter. The days are still turning but the season remains constant. All I see is ice. And it is here when multitudes of transparent ghosts flood in across the land. They move about like ants on a hill in what seems like complete disarray. But the longer I watch them, the more it looks like they are not wandering. They are patrolling. Guarding. Protecting.

The scene before me fades from my vision and with the blink of my eyes, I see the ghost withdrawing its hand from my head. It floats back to its position within the circle and they stare at me. My fear subsides and I begin to understand. These are the spirits of the land—its guardians. This is their land. And I no longer want to be here. I no longer want to explore and settle. I wish to no longer trespass upon their land.

As if they heard my thoughts, the spirits whisper and their ghostly forms flutter and vanish in the wind.

I tie off the main sail and take my position at the ships rudder. The sea is calm this morning and graces me with a favorable wind that pushes me eastward. Homeward. I look upon the luscious green land full of mountains, moss, and hot springs and cannot help but see the vision of many seasons rushing by in my mind. Yet it always fixates on the many years of winter. I take one last look back and see the land, nearly out of sight. What a glorious land it is. The Land of Ice. Now that I think of it, that makes a good name for this place. Iceland.

The Reign of Evil

Preview

The Reign of Evil *was first conceived in Curson's grade 6 classroom when he wrote a story for a writing contest. The idea grew far past the 1000 word limit but Curson kept with it. In what seemed like no time at all, a novel was born. Fast-forward several years later when Curson graduated high-school, he picked up the idea once more and properly wrote his childhood story that he had been carrying with him.*

Nidavia lies isolated—just what the King of Shadow needs to launch his conquest.

Alone, the nations of Nidavia stand powerless against the might of King Dosleum, his army, and the hordes of monsters at his command. The war has already begun, starting with the vulnerable nation of Penthiln.

Hawk and Falcon, two brothers named after their mysterious birthmarks, are thrown into the war when Dosleum forces invade their homeland. Their tale begins when their parents are captured.

Having lived on their small farm separated from the world for reasons known only to their parents, they pursue the mercenaries into the heart of Dosleum. There, they learn of their hidden past and uncover the mystery of their birthmarks.

Most importantly, Hawk and Falcon discover who they are and that the fate of Nidavia rests in their hands—the hands of two farmers.

Containing all the essentials for a fantasy novel, *The Reign of Evil* is a fast-paced read full of quests, dragons, monsters, and more battles that can be counted. Follow Hawk and Falcon's adventure as they do what they must to unite Nidavia and defeat King Dosleum.

PETER CURSON

The First Battle of Noltreydelm
(Excerpt)

Very soon, they could hear the sound of battle ahead of them. Through the constant sound of clanging armor could be heard clashes and screams—both in fury and in pain. It was not the first time Hawk and Falcon heard the noises of battle, but they had not yet grown accustomed to it. Though they did try very hard.

A soldier riding a horse and wearing armor similar to Rob's rode up to meet them. One of his captains. "General Rob! They have penetrated our defenses!"

"The Dosleum soldiers? How could they have done this so easily?"

"I cannot tell you, General, I have just arrived moments before you, and our soldiers are being forced back!"

"Okay men," the General shouted to all around him. "We will not let them retake this city! Go forth and slaughter all who stand against us!" And with that, the General was off with all his horsemen charging off behind him. There was not any fear in the general. It seemed to the brothers that his very being was comprised courage. In fact, every soldier seemed that way.

Hawk and Falcon looked to each other one last time and simultaneously they snapped the reins and rode towards the battle. The cavalry rounded one final corner, placing them on a rather wide street and there they saw the battle. Dosleum soldiers bombarded their way down the street meeting heavy resistance from the Fairence soldiers. It was a relentless attack. In mere seconds, General Rob smashed into the Dosleum forces and began his attack. And in only a few more, the two farmers from Penthlin would soon be in the middle of it as well.

The brothers hopelessly clung to their horses as their steeds crashed into the enemy, galloping through soldiers and trampling them as they went until they began to slow down. Hawk gripped his father's sword tightly, but held on to the reins even tighter. But then something happened that Hawk did not see coming. Suddenly, his horse fell from underneath him. He felt a harsh shove and catapulted forward. As he flew in the air, he collided with someone and fell to the ground. The impact hurt Hawk terribly, but he did not notice; he was face to face with a Dosleum soldier.

The soldier took hold of Hawk and tried to wrestle him off with both of his hands. He must have lost his weapon. But Hawk then realized that he, too, was wrestling back with both hands. The soldier began overpowering him. He raised Hawk into the air. They were both shouting while trying to fight against one another. Finally, the soldier threw Hawk off him. Hawk landed on his side with a crash. After opening his eyes from the fall, he saw a golden handle in front of his eyes. He quickly gripped his sword and instinctively swung upwards without looking. The sword connected. Hawk saw the soldier as he fell to his knees; a gaping wound pouring blood marred his chest. With no more strength left in him, the soldier gave into his wounds and collapsed fully onto Hawk. Hawk squirmed from underneath the corpse. Without taking his eyes

PETER CURSON

off the man he just killed, he slid backwards from underneath his deceased enemy and did not stop shuffling backwards until he hit a wall. Quickly turning his head, he saw a doorway beside him. He darted for the door, his legs nearly giving in, and entered the house.

Everything in the house was overturned and trashed. Hawk took a moment to stop and catch his breath. Then he heard crashing footsteps from behind him. Hawk spun on his heels again swinging his sword. A hand caught onto his arm before it could connect. Hawk's gaze caught up and he saw Falcon holding onto him.

"Falcon!"

"Hawk, are you okay? There's blood on you!"

"It is not mine. At least not all of it. I am fine! What about you?"

Before Falcon could answer, a loud and gruesome noise filled the air. A shout of some sort. The brothers flinched at the noise and everything outside quieted as if the soldiers had stopped fighting, which was, for a part, true.

"Did you hear that?"

"Yeah, what was—"

Now the noise came again but louder. It was no longer a shout, but a guttural roar. The brothers clung to each other as they looked back through the doorway to the street outside. All they could see were Fairence soldiers but they had stopped fighting, they had stopped moving entirely, except they were shaking. Their gazes fixated further down the street. Nothing happened as the brothers listened. They heard movement from down the street as if a large amount of people were advancing towards them, yet the Fairence soldiers did nothing to stop them. Every few seconds, the brothers thought they could hear something, some kind of growl, but could not place what it was and they did not risk speaking about it either. It was something deep, a sound a snarling animal might make.

But if it was an animal, it was something they had never encountered.

Their running imaginations were cut short when the Fairence soldiers began to slowly walk backwards. Backwards. Whatever was on the road that neared was sucking the very courage from the most courageous men on Nidavia. Suddenly, they heard the roar once again, even louder this time. But countless more roars answered. And the Fairence soldiers ran.

Falcon shoved Hawk backwards not waiting to find out what drove the Fairence soldiers to falter and turn tail. "Quick, behind the table."

Hawk managed to spin around and saw an overturned table in one of the corners. He flung himself over and Falcon followed. They knelt behind the table and held their weapons close. The roaring did not stop. But the sounds of battle began once more. This time it was different. The sounds of agony intensified and the sound of weaponry diminished. The battle progressed rapidly towards them. All the progress they had just made was being undone at such an alarming rate until the battle was right outside the door. Hawk and Falcon could hear the roars and the howls more clearly now. They were dreadful and painful even to listen to. Could a human mouth even utter such horrible sounds?

The brothers listened intently on the battle outside until something drew them out of it. A heavy footstep landed just inside of the house. And then another. Someone—or something—had entered. Falcon looked to Hawk whose eyes were squeezed shut. He tried to listen but the sound of his heartbeat was too loud in his ears. Whatever had entered took another step closer and then it started growling, a low and rasping gnarl that made the brothers tremble. Another footstep. And another. It was nearly at the table. The growling stopped and in its place, sniffing.

Hawk's eyes opened and met Falcon's. He could see his

brother was scared, but he saw something building inside of him. Falcon did not want to wait around to see what happened next. His grip on his axe tightened. Hawk gripped his sword as well and nodded. The table abruptly moved and flew away from the brothers revealing them. They both stood up to attack but immediately froze when they saw what had just thrown the table across the room.

Glossary of Characters

Æsir

Balder	Most beloved of the Æsir Son of Odin Brother of Hod
Heimdall	Guardian of Bifrost
Hoenir	Sent to Vanaheim at the end of the Æsir-Vanir war Brother of Mímir
Magni	Son of Thor Brother of Modi
Mímir	Sent to Vanaheim at the end of the Æsir-Vanir war Brother of Hoenir
Modi	Son of Thor Brother of Magni
Odin	Chief of the Æsir
Thor	God of Thunder, God of War Son of Odin

Týr	God of War, God of Justice
Vali	Son of Odin Brother of Vidar
Vidar	Son of Odin Brother of Vali

Ásynjur

Frigg	Queen of the Ásynjur Wife of Odin
Nanna	Wife of Balder
Sif	Wife of Thor

Jötnar

Angrboda	Wife of Loki Mother of Fenrir, Jormungand, and Hél
Fenrisulfr (Fenrir, Fen)	The Wolf Brother of Jormungand and Hél Son of Loki
Hati	Son of Fenrir Brother of Sköll

PETER CURSON

Hél	The Dark Ruler of Hélheim Sister of Jormungand and Fenrir Daughter of Loki
Hyrrokkin	Wife of Fenrir
Jormungand (Jor)	The Midgard Serpent Brother of Fenrir and Hél Son of Loki
Loki	The Trickster Blood-brother of Odin Father of Fenrir, Jormungand, and Hél
Modgud	Guardian of the River Gjöll
Sköll	Son of Fenrir Brother of Hati

Vanir

Frey	King of the Elves Brother of Freya
Freya	Queen of the Vanir Sister of Frey

Humans

Alf	King of Svealand
Einherjar	Dead human warriors who live eternally in Valhalla
Fairhair	King of Norvay
Gautar	The people of Gautland
Hjordis	Mother of Sigurd Wife to King Alf
Kára	First lover of Fenrir Lost her status as Valkyrie when Thor caused her fall during battle
Matunaagd	Of the Sko-ko-mish tribe in Xwayxway Brother of Megedagik
Megedagik	Of the Sko-ko-mish tribe in Xwayxway Brother of Matunaagd
Signy	Sister of Sigmund
Sigurd	Son of Sigmund and Hjordis
Sko-ko-mish	The people inhabiting the lands around Xwayxway (present day Skwxwú7mesh, or Squamish)

PETER CURSON

Svear	The people of Svealand

Animals

Freki	Odin's wolf
Garm	Hél's hound
Geri	Odin's wolf
Huginn	Odin's raven Spies on Midgard
Muninn	Odin's raven Spies on Midgard
Nidhogg	Dragon in the roots of Yggdrasil
Ratatosk	Squirrel in Yggdrasil
Sleipnir	Odin's eight-legged horse
The Eagle	Eagle at the top of Yggdrasil

Dwarves

Fafnir	Son of King Hreidmar Brother of Otr and Regin Turned into a dragon by the curse of Andvaranaut

Hreidmar	King of the Dwarves
Otr	Son of King Hreidmar Brother of Fafnir and Regin
Regin	Son of King Hreidmar Brother of Fafnir and Otr

Glossary of Locations

Alba	Present day Scotland
Alfheim	One of the Nine Worlds Home to the elves
Asgard	One of the Nine Worlds Home to the Æsir gods
Bærin	An Æsir town
Bifrost	The Rainbow Bridge Connects Asgard to Midgard
Birca	Trading center in Svealand (present day Birka, Sweden)
Constantinople	Present day Istanbul, Turkey
England	Present day England, United Kingdom
Francia	Present day France
Gautland	One of the historical Lands of Sweden (present day southern Sweden)
Gjöll	A river in Hélheim

Hälsingborg	Port town in Gautland (present day Helsingborg, Sweden)
Hämnd	Town in Svealand
Hélheim	One of the Nine Worlds Home to the dead
Innangard	The capital of Asgard
Ireland	Present day Ireland
Jötunheim	One of the Nine Worlds Home to the Jötnar
Karlstad	Trading town in Svealand (present day Karlstad, Sweden)
Lund	Town in Gautland (present day Lund, Sweden)
Midgard	One of the Nine Worlds Home to the humans
Mímir's Well	A well within Yggdrasil's roots, whose water contains much wisdom
Muspelheim	One of the Nine Worlds All-consuming fire
Nidavellir	One of the Nine Worlds Home to the dwarves
Niflheim	One of the Nine Worlds All-consuming ice

PETER CURSON

Norvay	Present day Norway
Oförtjänt	Village in Svealand
Rome	Present day Rome, Italy
Svealand	One of the historical Lands of Sweden (present day central Sweden)
Trelleborg	Town in Gautland (present day Trelleborg, Sweden)
Turgu	Trading city (present day Turku, Finland)
Uppåkra	Town in Gautland (present day Uppakra, Sweden)
Urd's Well	From which Yggdrasil grows Where the Three Norns reside
Valhalla	Odin's Hall Home of the Einherjar
Vanaheim	One of the Nine Worlds Home to the Vanir gods
Xwayxway	A Sko-ko-mish village (present day Vancouver, Canada)
Yggdrasil	The World Tree

Glossary of Norse Words

Andvaranaut	A gold ring that carries a curse for all who possess it
Ás (pl. Æsir)	A god of Asgard
Ásynja (pl. Ásynjur)	A goddess of Asgard
Gleipnir	The fetter used to secure Fenrir. It is comprised of: 1. The sound of a cat's footfall 2. The beard of a woman 3. The roots of a mountain 4. The sinews of a bear 5. The breath of a fish 6. The spittle of a bird
Gungnir	Odin's Spear.
Holmgang	A duel fought to settle disputes.
Innangard	"Within the enclosure" The concept of lawfulness and order
Jötunn (pl. Jötnar)	A giant of Jötunheim
Mjölnir	Thor's Hammer

Ragnarök	The apocalypse and new beginning
Ragr	Unmanly, effeminate
Seid	Shamanism or shamanistic magic involved with seeing and altering destiny.
Skald	One who composes and recites poems, typically about heroes and their tales
Utangard	"Beyond the enclosure" The concept of lawlessness and chaos
Vana (pl. Vanir)	A god of Vanaheim
Veslingr	Puny wretch

Glossary of Other Words

Amarok	Giant wolf in Inuit mythology
U'ligan	Kwakwaka'wakw word for "wolf"
Varulv	Swedish word for "werewolf"
Vuko-dlak	Slavic word for "werewolf"
Werwulf	Old English word for "werewolf"